"Let's ~~f~~ [we just ru~~b each other~~ up] the wrong way.

"I don't trust you and I don't like—"

Reaching out, he put a long finger on her lips. "Don't say you don't like me, Bryony, because I know you do. You're just afraid of trusting your heart again." Gently he ran his fingertips over her lips with a light caressing touch. "We'll see each other again...."

"Would you care to be the guest author at a readers' party in Sicily?" That question and my acceptance led me to an island of beauty and contrasts—the modern holiday resorts against the primitiveness of Etna's smoking crater; the crowded towns and the peace of a garden—to the warmth of the sun and even greater warmth and hospitality of the many Sicilians I met. I shall go back there again, for a long and leisurely holiday...."

—*SALLY WENTWORTH*

Books by Sally Wentworth

HARLEQUIN PRESENTS

1550—THE GOLDEN GREEK
1572—STORMY VOYAGE
1605—THE WAYWARD WIFE
1634—MIRRORS OF THE SEA
1668—YESTERDAY'S AFFAIR
1701—PRACTICE TO DECEIVE

SALLY WENTWORTH

Sicilian Spring

Harlequin Books

TORONTO • NEW YORK • LONDON
AMSTERDAM • PARIS • SYDNEY • HAMBURG
STOCKHOLM • ATHENS • TOKYO • MILAN
MADRID • WARSAW • BUDAPEST • AUCKLAND

ISBN 0-373-18601-0

SICILIAN SPRING

Copyright © 1993 by Sally Wentworth.

First North American Publication 1995.

Printed in U.S.A.

CHAPTER ONE

WEDDINGS were supposed to be the start of a new life, for the bride and groom, but this one was also destined to change the life of one of the guests. A very reluctant guest. For Bryony Ferrers the invitation came at just the wrong time. She had recently broken up with her boyfriend after nearly two years and the last thing she wanted to do was to go to someone else's wedding. It was a family wedding, too, her cousin Georgina's; and from past experience Bryony knew that her relations would have no hesitation in asking about *her* prospects of becoming a bride. Prospects that were now definitely minus zero!

She shuddered at the thought and tried to wriggle out of the invitation, but there was a martial light in her mother's eyes and a determined thrust to her father's jaw which told Bryony there was no getting out of this one. As their only daughter, very beloved, and, in their eyes, very beautiful, she was to go and be shown off to the family and the new in-laws.

The wedding was at the beginning of March when you could reasonably expect frost or even snow, but it turned out to be unseasonably warm and sunny, which didn't match Bryony's mood at all. Georgina looked lovely, as all brides should, gazing at her new husband with adoring eyes as they walked back up the aisle. A pang of envious jealousy shot through Bryony's heart, but then she saw the smug smile of triumph on the groom's face and her emotion swiftly changed to hatred of the entire male sex. Rotten lot, marrying women just so that they could get an unpaid servant for life. She was *glad* she and Jeff had broken up. And she was going to make darn sure that she never let another man get that close to her again. At least now she could lead her own life. But then Bryony realised that she hadn't the slightest idea what kind of life she wanted to lead and her heart filled with dismay again.

At the reception at a local hotel, Bryony did her best to elude her relatives but wasn't allowed to do so, her parents taking a firm grip on her arms as they went from group to group to say hello. Those who knew about her failed romance gave her sympathetic looks and tactfully avoided the subject, which was almost harder to take than those who didn't know or had forgotten — mostly her male relatives — and came straight out with, 'And when are we going to be invited to *your* wedding, Bryony?'

It wasn't until after the buffet meal had been eaten, the speeches made, and the cake cut, that she was able to get herself a glass of champagne and steal away to a small room further down the corridor. It looked as if it was sometimes used for cards from the folded tables in a corner. All Bryony cared about was that it was empty. She sat in a deep window seat overlooking the garden, leaned back against the wall and kicked off her shoes, then took a long drink. Peace at last!

Two minutes later the door opened and she groaned inwardly, praying that it wouldn't be one of the wedding guests. It's not my day, she thought as a middle-aged woman she remembered having seen at the reception came in. But the woman looked a little put out to find her there and Bryony recognised a kindred spirit. 'Don't mind me,' she said, lifting her glass in greeting. 'I'm not in the mood for weddings, either.'

The woman smiled and dropped into a deep arm-chair. 'One always feel so antisocial if you don't stand up all the time at these affairs.' And she, too, kicked off her shoes.

High-heeled and expensive-looking Italian shoes, Bryony noticed. And the woman's clothes were also well-designed but couldn't hide the fact that her figure was definitely matronly. Racking her brain, Bryony tried to think who she was; she certainly wasn't a relation but there was a vague recollection of having met her before.

It seemed the woman was having the same problem because she frowned and said, 'You're — er — '

'Bryony Ferrers. Georgina's cousin.'

'Oh, of course. I should have remembered. I met you at Georgina's eighteenth birthday party.'

'That was some time ago,' Bryony said tactfully. 'I'm afraid I don't quite remember your connection with the family.'

'Oh, I'm not a relation. I'm Georgina's godmother. I was at school with her mother.'

'Oh, yes, of course.' Which put her age at around fifty but didn't give Bryony much help with her name.

Guessing her thoughts, the woman looked at her and smiled. 'I am the Contessa Henrietta del Cavalleri.' She smiled again when she saw the startled expression on Bryony's face, and added, 'Etta, for short.'

'That's Italian, isn't it?'

'Yes, my husband was an Italian.'

'Was?' Bryony asked hesitantly.

'Yes, he died nine months ago.'

'Oh, I'm sorry.'

The Contessa gave a slight, resigned shrug. 'Antonio was much older than I. And at least I know that I made his last years happy.'

'You weren't married very long, then?'

'Five years. We met at a party.' She gave a reminiscent smile. 'I always seem to meet like-minded people at parties. And almost as soon as I met him I decided that I wanted to marry Antonio. That was after I found out that he was a rich widower, of course.' She raised a well-groomed eyebrow at Bryony. 'Does that shock you?'

Bryony grinned, liking the Contessa more by the minute. 'Of course not. Did you become a stepmother?'

'Luckily, no,' Etta said feelingly. 'Antonio had no children — not legitimate ones at least. I wouldn't be at all surprised if he had some illegitimate children around somewhere, but if he had they were kept discreetly in the background. They know how to do these things in Italy.'

'And were you married before, Contessa?' Bryony asked, becoming intrigued by her companion.

'Oh, please call me Etta; Contessa sounds so stuffy.' The older woman paused for a moment, giving Bryony an assessing glance, then said, 'No, I wasn't married before. But I have had — and enjoyed — one or two long-standing romantic affairs. I suppose nowadays you would call them meaningful relationships.' She saw Bryony's face tighten and added ruefully, 'Now I really have shocked you.'

'No.' Bryony shook her head. 'It's just that — well, I was involved in a "meaningful relationship" myself until recently.'

'Did you break it off?'

'I don't know, to be honest,' Bryony admitted with a perplexed shake of her head. 'Things had been getting pretty uptight. I began to suspect that he'd been seeing someone else but I was afraid of bringing it out in the open. Partly because I knew he'd accuse me of not trusting him, and partly,' she added musingly, 'because I was afraid that he might admit it. Then I found an earring that wasn't mine in his jacket pocket and everything just erupted. We had an almighty row.'

'And did he accuse you of not trusting him?'

'Of course. And he refused to say whether there was someone else or not.'

'Typical,' Etta said sympathetically. 'He wanted to put you in the wrong. So what happened?'

'We both walked out at the same time. I went home to mother; I don't know where Jeff went. The flat was left empty. I waited for him to beg me to come back and I suppose he waited for me to beg him to come back. But — well, neither of us did.'

'Then you were obviously right to part,' Etta said briskly. 'In a year or so you will look back on all this and think it very funny.'

She spoke with such assurance that Bryony smiled. 'I love your attitude. Everyone else who knows treats me as if I'm a grief-stricken widow or something.' Then she realised what she'd said and added quickly, 'Oh, I'm sorry, I——'

'Please, don't apologise. I was very fond of Antonio and sad when he died. I grieved for him and still do when I'm alone, but now I'm ready to look to the future again.'

'Well, as a rich widow. . .'

Etta's eyebrows drew into a frown. 'That's what I thought. But unfortunately things didn't work out quite the way I expected.'

Bryony was about to ask her why but for the first time realised that she was talking to a comparative stranger and someone of her parents' generation at that; Etta had been so open and friendly that she had been chatting to her almost as a contemporary. Now Bryony drew back, not wanting to be nosy, although she would have loved to know, but it was up to Etta to tell her if she wanted to, not for her to ask.

After a few moments lost in thought, Etta glanced at Bryony's now empty glass. 'What we need is some more champagne to drown our sorrows.' There was a service phone in the room and Etta asked for a waiter, and when he came had no hesitation in telling him to bring in a bottle of champagne from the wedding reception, slipping him a tip when he did so. 'This will make us feel better,' she announced, filling their glasses. 'Now, tell me about yourself.'

'There's so much, it will take ages.'

Etta gave her an approving look. 'That's much better than the "There's nothing to tell" answer one always gets from young girls. I like a positive approach. Go on.'

'I'm the only child of doting parents,' Bryony told her with a grin. 'Spoilt rotten and indulged in everything I ever wanted to have or do.'

'But you've survived despite it,' Etta said with a smile.

'I think so. I managed to pass my exams and go to college even though they were petrified of pushing me and letting me know how much it mattered to them. In case I felt pressured, I suppose. When I was about twelve a friend and I read a book about a girl who was a chalet maid in an up-market ski resort, and we decided that it would be a terribly glamorous thing to do. So we took languages and went to cordon bleu classes, and the first winter after leaving college got jobs at a chalet in the Italian Alps.'

'You speak Italian?' Etta asked in surprise.

'Yes, but not as fluently as someone like yourself who's lived there, of course.'

'My dear girl, I hardly speak a word. Antonio spoke such good English that it wasn't necessary. Although now I rather wish I'd bothered to learn. But I'm interrupting you; do go on.'

'It was terribly hard work,' Bryony told her. 'Not really a glamour job at all, but after a couple of months we got the hang of it and found some time to go skiing and join in the après-ski. And it was then I met Jeff. He was on holiday with some friends, but staying at a hotel, not the chalet. We fell for each other straight away. And he actually persuaded the people who had taken the chalet to swap accommodation with his group so that he could see more of me. Don't you think that's terribly romantic?'

'Very. And very convenient for him, too,' Etta said drily.

Bryony laughed. 'Yes, I suppose it was. My friend, Caroline, hit it off with one of Jeff's friends and we did hardly any work that week; we were skiing on the slopes all day and ate out in the evenings.'

'And when they all went home?' Etta prompted as Bryony became lost in recollection.

'Well, I didn't delude myself into thinking that it would be more than a holiday thing, but a few weeks later Jeff turned up again, but alone this time. He'd taken over the whole chalet but under a different name so that I didn't even know he was coming until he arrived. And he'd booked a hotel room for Caroline so that we could have the place to ourselves.' She sighed. 'He really did the most romantic things.'

'And I don't suppose you did much skiing.'

'Well, it did snow a lot that week,' Bryony explained excusingly. Then she laughed. 'You must admit he had style.'

'And swept you off your feet; I know. But was it the man you fell in love with or the romantic excitement of it all?' Etta asked shrewdly.

'Well, it lasted two years.'

'And you didn't become bored?'

'I never get bored. There's always so many things to do and see, especially when you live in London. I went on art and antiques courses, things like that. And whenever Jeff had to go away on business I always went with him.'

'You didn't have a job?'

Bryony flushed. 'Well, no. Jeff didn't want me to. He liked me to be available to meet him for lunch and go away with him, as I said.' She paused. 'I suppose you think that's wrong?' She said with a slight challenge in her tone.

'Good heavens, no! If a man wants to keep you, then let him, I always say. After all, if you'd been married he would have had to keep you, wouldn't he?'

'Yes, I suppose so.'

'Then why should you expect to live differently just because you're an — er — partner instead of a wife?'

'A question of pride, perhaps?'

'Nonsense!' Etta said roundly. '*Your* commitment was the same, and so should his have been. And I'm not surprised that he wanted to show you off; you're a very attractive girl.'

'Thank you.' Bryony smiled. 'You know, you're very good for my morale. I could never talk about it like this with my parents; they tried so hard to be terribly modern about it and like Jeff, but every time my mother saw us you could almost see her longing to ask when we were going to get married.'

'But the subject didn't arise? Or only recently, perhaps?'

'You're right,' Bryony admitted ruefully. 'I had made noises about getting engaged.'

'A mistake,' Etta obseved. 'It reminds young men that there's such a thing in the world as responsibility and a mortgage. That they might have to grow up.'

'You think that's why we split up? Jeff wanted to make the break, perhaps even subconsciously, and was pushing us into a row?'

'Well, weren't you pushing him to find out?'

Bryony sat up straight as she looked at Etta. 'Maybe you're right at that.'

'Of course I am. I have vast experience with men,' Etta said comfortably.

Looking at her, Bryony didn't doubt it. Etta was still smart and had a good bone-structure, even if her figure was rather rounded. But it was her vitality and something about her that immediately made you feel at ease that was her biggest attraction. Perhaps it was charm, that elusive and longed-for quality.

'And what are you going to do now?' Etta asked.

'Find a job somewhere, I suppose. Although it might be difficult after a couple of years of not doing anything in particular. Employers like people who're experienced nowadays, and there are so many people out of work that they can afford to pick and choose. After all, what qualifications do I have except being able to speak French and Italian?'

'But you can cook. And you have taken art courses, you say?'

'Yes, but who would want someone like that?'

Etta leant forward in her chair. 'As a matter of fact, *I* might.'

'You, Etta? But I——'

'I have a villa in Sicily that I'm thinking of turning into a hotel; a very exclusive one, you understand, with just a few guests. But I need someone I can trust to help run it. Someone who speaks Italian, can cook, and is good at meeting people. Does that ring a bell?'

Bryony stared at her, opening her mouth to make a hundred objections but not knowing where to start.

Taking advantage of her confusion, Etta said, 'What do you have to lose? You have no other plans, and somehow I can't see you wanting to live with your parents again—not after having lived away for two years. And it would give you a chance to get over Jeff.

There would be lots of new interests, new places to see. And think of the climate! I would pay you a good wage, and if it works out, if the hotel becomes successful, then you could perhaps have a percentage of the profits.' Her voice filled with enthusiasm. 'We could build up a reputation so that we would be in the best guide books, and even——' She broke off as Bryony held up a hand.

'Hey! Don't get carried away. I—I think it sounds wonderful. Just what I need. But we've hardly met. Are you sure that I'm the right person for what you want?'

'Well, if it doesn't work out then you could always leave, or I could always fire you,' Etta said practically.

Bryony burst into laughter, but her eyes were shining as she said, 'Well, I'd certainly like to discuss it some more.'

'Then we need some more champagne.'

'I don't mean now. I think we both ought to think it over first and then meet again to talk about it further.'

Etta smiled. 'You mean when we're both completely sober. Very sensible.'

'How long are you in England?'

'Another week. I'm staying at the Savoy in London. How about meeting me for lunch there on Monday?'

'That will be fine.'

Etta put on her shoes and got to her feet. 'I suppose we'd better go back to the wedding. You can tell your parents you were being very kind and keeping me company.'

Bryony laughed as she, too, rose. She gave her companion a bemused look. 'How strange that we should meet like this.'

'Perhaps it's fate. I'm a great believer in fate.' Etta took her hand. 'I hope that you'll accept my offer,

Bryony. I liked you at once and I think that this could work out well for both of us.'

Bryony almost impulsively accepted there and then, her mind filled with eager excitement, but she had learnt a little caution since Jeff, and merely said, 'I'll look forward to Monday.'

The whole of the next day Bryony was expecting a call from Etta to say that she'd had second thoughts and was almost surprised when the day ended and the call hadn't come. Deciding not to say anything to her parents until after her second meeting, Bryony made her way to the Savoy the next morning, still feeling that Etta would have changed her mind. But the Contessa greeted her warmly and was just as keen for Bryony to join her in the venture. So keen in fact that Bryony found herself almost arguing against it. 'You haven't sampled my cooking,' she protested.

'You got your certificates, didn't you?'

'Yes, I've brought them along for you to see,' Bryony replied, taking them from her bag.

Etta waved them aside with a well-manicured hand. 'Cooking is like swimming and driving—once you've learnt you never forget. To me the most important thing is that we get along well together, and I'm sure we will. And that you're reliable, of course, but only time will prove that.'

'But I have no experience of hotel work.'

'Nor have I, but I rather think that will be an advantage because we'll see it from the guests' point of view and run it accordingly,' Etta replied with supreme optimism.

'That doesn't sound terribly businesslike,' Bryony commented.

'Well, we won't be exactly cheap. And we'll make everyone so welcome and comfortable that they'll come back again and again,' Etta said with assurance.

Bryony believed her, but she still had to sell the idea
to her parents, so she said, 'I have lots of questions to
ask, and I think it would be a good idea, for both our
sakes, if we worked out some sort of contract.'

So Bryony asked her questions and had any reser-
vations swept aside by Etta's overwhelming enthusiasm
and optimism. But they worked out a contract on the
back of an envelope, Bryony promising to stay for at
least six months and Etta, in turn, pledging to pay her
fare to Sicily, a basic wage and her keep, and then a
percentage of the profits after one year if she stayed on.

'I take it I'll live at the villa?' And when Etta nodded,
'And you'll be living there too, of course?'

'Most of the time, although I may have to go away
for a few days now and then. I have lots of friends,' she
said obliquely. 'I'm sure many of them will want to stay
at our hotel.'

'I can't wait to start,' Bryony said enthusiastically.

'That's good, because I would like you to come with
me when I go back to Sicily next week.'

'Next week! Good heavens.'

'Does it present a problem?'

Bryony laughed. 'Not really, no. It's just the speed
at which all this has happened. Forty-eight hours ago I
didn't even know you and now you've changed my life.'
She grinned again. 'As a matter of fact I rather like it.'

Etta nodded. 'You're the type of girl who isn't afraid
to grab an opportunity.'

'The way I grabbed Jeff, you mean. But look at the
way that turned out,' she said on a pessimistic note.

'Ah, yes, but he was a man, and they're seldom a
hundred per cent reliable — unless handled properly,
that is.'

Intrigued, Bryony said, 'One day you must tell me
the story of your life.'

Etta's eyes sparkled with amusement. 'One day—when I've had enough champagne—I might.'

The next week was one of the busiest in Bryony's life. First she had to tell her parents and convince them that she was doing 'the right thing'. She expected and got a lot of discussion—not argument because they always tried to see her point of view. She was aware that they both, either separately or together, phoned Etta when she was out and might even have gone to see her, because at first they'd seemed against the idea but then changed.

'Perhaps it would be a good thing for you to get away for a while,' her mother said. 'It will help you get over Jeff if you meet new people.'

By 'people' her mother of course meant men, but Bryony smiled and kissed her. 'I'm sure it will. I'm really looking forward to it.'

'And perhaps we'll come over and be your first guests in the hotel. We've never been to Sicily,' her father put in.

'Great!' Bryony exclaimed, meaning it. 'Then I'll be able to practise on you.'

Completely ignorant of how a hotel should be run, Bryony bought some books on the subject and, with the supreme optimism of youth, rang one of the top hotels in London and asked if she could come and see how it was managed. Perhaps amused by her certainty that he would want to help her, the manager allowed her to come even at such short notice and she spent hours being passed from one department to another, making copious notes. All the areas—kitchens, house-keeping, bars, restaurants—were interesting, but Bryony found that she was especially surprised by the promotions department, whose young female manager overwhelmed her with ideas. Bryony went away with her mind reeling. Many of the ideas, of course, would be quite unsuitable for the kind of hotel that Etta had described, but, if they ever found that they needed to attract custom, then some of them could definitely be used.

That evening Bryony rang Etta to excitedly tell her about it, but Etta laughingly stopped her. 'My dear girl, I thoroughly admire your enterprise, but I'm afraid I'm just going out to dinner with an old friend so you'll have to save it all for a while. Tell me on the plane; we'll have lots of time to talk then.'

Her mother helped her to pack, becoming almost as excited as she was, and said, 'You must take all your cookery books with you, of course. You'll need those.'

Bryony looked up from the drawer she was going through. 'Yes.' But she said it slowly, remembering that the books, and a lot of other things, were still at the flat she had shared with Jeff.

Her mother gave her one glance and understood immediately. 'We'll go round there together tomorrow morning and get them,' she said firmly.

But when they drove round to the flat the next day Bryony hesitated before turning to her mother and saying, 'Would you mind if I went up alone? Just — just for a few minutes.'

'Jeff isn't likely to be there, is he?'

'No, I'm sure he'll be at work. But even so, I'd. . .'

'Of course,' her mother said briskly. 'Why don't you go and pack all your things and I'll call back for you in an hour?'

'Yes, please. That would be fine.' Bryony smiled, thanking her stars for such an understanding parent.

Even though she knew he wouldn't be there, Bryony felt strangely nervous as she turned her key in the door. There were no letters on the mat; she had had her mail re-directed and she supposed that Jeff must have done the same. But there were marks in the dust that layered the carpet. So he must have been here, and quite recently. It seemed strange now to walk through the rooms of her other life, one that was now over. Her mind filled with memories, most of them happy ones, and she suddenly wondered again if she had done the wrong thing. Perhaps she shouldn't have walked out, perhaps she should have called him and begged him to come back. If she had they might have been living here again now, as happy as they had once been. It wasn't too late, she could still call, phone him right this minute.

But the dust and the emptiness told her that it was. Jeff hadn't even come back here to live, hadn't waited for her to return.

Many of Jeff's things were gone but there were still some of his clothes in the wardrobe, his books in the bookcases, and his CDs by the player. The rent on the flat had been paid in advance and still had some time to run; there hadn't been any need to rush to break up what had been their home. On a table there was a large framed photo of them both, taken in the days when they had first been together, when they had been completely happy with each other. Jeff hadn't taken it with him. Well, nor would she. Her resolve suddenly strengthened, Bryony began to pack the suitcases and boxes she had brought with her, filling them with everything that belonged to her. The flat had come furnished so there was none of that to worry about, but she had made and bought things to adorn it, working and choosing with loving care, all of which seemed now to be wasted. But she didn't see why she should leave them for Jeff or some future tenant.

By the time her mother came to collect her Bryony was waiting, everything packed and ready by the door, but as the bell rang Bryony was unable to stop herself going back to the table, picking up the photograph and thrusting it deep into one of the boxes.

At the airport her luggage was well over the weight limit, but so was Etta's, for she seemed to have done a great deal of shopping while she was in London.

'Have you been buying things for the hotel?' Bryony asked as the cases disappeared down the conveyor belt.

Etta chuckled richly. 'I suppose you could say that; after all, as the proprietor I must look the part.'

She looked good now, in a dark grey outfit with a bright red scarf at the neck and a matching hat. Bryony looked pretty good, too, in olive-green, her slim figure and clear, long-lashed grey eyes, her fair hair drawn back from the face to emphasise the good bone-structure, attracting the glances of many of their fellow travellers.

Finding some seats, Etta began to tell Bryony about the concert and a couple of plays she'd seen while she was in London, and they were still disucssing them when their flight was called. The plane took off on time and they relaxed into their club-class seats, the steward bringing them glasses of champagne.

'I suppose we ought to drink to the success of the hotel,' Etta remarked.

'Of course.' Bryony raised her glass. 'Here's to a fantastic future. What will you call it — the Hotel Cavalleri?'

The champagne must have gone down the wrong way, because Etta choked over her drink and coughed, her face losing colour. 'No. No, I don't think so. Something more — neutral than that, I think. We'll have to think of somethng.'

'It's going to be such fun,' Bryony declared. 'It all seems too good to be true.'

'Ye-es.' Etta gave her a rather strange look, seemed

about to say something, then changed her mind. 'You were going to tell me about your visit to the hotel.'

Bryony's eager description and the discussion that followed it, interrupted by a meal and more drinks, lasted until the end of the flight. The day was almost gone when Bryony had her first glimpse of Sicily through the plane window. The island, golden in the rays of the setting sun, lay below her, surrounded by the deep blue of the sea. The very heart of the Mediterranean. As the plane began to descend towards the runway, Bryony's heart filled with a kind of relieved excitement; there was no going back, the old life was definitely behind her now, the new one about to begin.

There was a car and chauffeur waiting to meet them, the car a large Rolls-Royce, grey and a few years old, the chauffeur a short Italian, grey-clad and about forty years old.

'This is Giovanni,' Etta introduced. 'He and his wife, Maria, look after the house for me.'

'*Buona sera*,' Bryony said with a smile, returning the man's greeting and shaking his hand.

He looked pleased, and his smile only slipped slightly when he saw the mound of luggage he had to pack into the car.

It was a long drive from the airport and soon grew dark. Bryony could see little except when they went through the narrow streets of a town. The cafés they passed seemed to be busy but it wasn't warm enough yet for people to sit outside. Leaving the town, they went through some open country, turned off the main road into a narrow lane and went through a high, arched gateway, the metal gates opening electrically before them, then up a wide drive leading to the villa, and a welcoming light over the deep-set, double wooden doors.

Etta turned to Bryony. 'Welcome to the Villa

Cavalleri,' she said formally, then laughed, 'Home at last.'

Inside, the villa was much as Bryony expected, with marble floors, white-painted walls, and rich, heavy furniture. But the room weren't too large or the ceilings too high, so that there was also a homely feel about it. Giovanni's wife, Maria, came hurrying to meet them, greeting Etta with a smile that held genuine warmth. 'Welcome home, Contessa.'

'Thank you, Maria, it's good to be here. Have there been any—problems while I've been away?' With just a trace of anxiety in her voice, Bryony noticed.

'No, *signora*, all has been well.'

'Good.' Etta's face cleared and she smiled as she turned to Bryony. 'This is Signorina Ferrers whom I told you about on the phone. You'll be pleased to know that she speaks Italian.'

Bryony shook hands and insisted on helping to carry her cases up to her room. It was a pretty room, on the second floor, but she had only time to change before the gong sounded for dinner. She and Etta ate alone in a smallish dining-room, the two staff waiting on them and serving food that Maria had prepared. It was good and wholesome but definitely not up to cordon bleu standard. After dinner they had coffee in the drawing-room, a large room with comfortable settees, but then Etta declared that she was tired after the journey.

'I'll show you over the house tomorrow,' she promised. 'And there are—things I must tell you. But not tonight. I'm going to bed. Stay up later if you want to, of course.'

But Bryony, too, went up to her room, although she wasn't used to going bed that early, and lay awake for a while, looking up at the strange ceiling, wondering what tomorrow would bring.

It brought a shaft of morning sunlight that woke her

early, around seven o'clock. Full of eager anticipation, Bryony jumped out of bed and went over to the window, pulling back the heavy curtains to look out. The garden was beautiful, full of flowers that wouldn't be out for at least another month back in England, dew glistening on the grass of lush green lawns. A high wall surrounded the garden, but beyond it Bryony glimpsed the line of the sea on the horizon, shimmering so brightly in the early sunlight that it hurt her eyes. She gave a gasp of sheer delight and hurried to shower and dress, pulling on jeans and a sweatshirt, leaving her hair loose, her face unmade-up as she ran out of her room.

The stairs led down to the first floor where all was quiet and widened into a grand staircase as they descended to the main hall. It was so early that she expected everyone to be still in bed and was surprised by the sound of someone moving about in the area where she guessed the kitchen to be. Maria and Giovanni must be early risers, too. At the front door, Bryony hesitated, wondering whether she ought to unbolt it, but then she remembered that there were French doors leading off the back of the hall on to a terrace, so she let herself out by those instead.

Even this early the sun was warm. Bryony lifted her face to it as she wandered round the garden, finding the swimming-pool and a flight of steps that led to a rose garden, the plants already bursting with new leaf, and beyond that a walled vegetable garden that was rather overgrown. There was a sunken garden, too, with a semi-circular stone seat in an arbour, a place that would be a sun-trap later in the year, and a tennis court with a sagging net, overlooked by a big conservatory furnished with wicker chairs and tables where the non-players could sit. But the place looked as if it hadn't been used for a long time, the glass windows were dirty and the floor covered in dust and dead leaves. Like a deserted house, Bryony thought, and wondered if Etta had used the conservatory since her husband had died.

The whole garden had a neglected air and would have to be worked on before they opened the hotel, but the villa, with its pale ochre-coloured walls and pantiled roof, its square tower covered with creeper at the far corner, had great potential, marvellous potential. I could be happy here, she thought, the warmth of the sun filling her with well-being. Walking round the house, Bryony came to the driveway at the front and noticed a small building a little distance away, nearer the arched gateway whose gates were now firmly closed. Curiously she walked towards it and, finding the door unlocked, walked in. It was a chapel, with a beautifully carved altar facing her and wooden pews on either side. Leaving the door open, she walked forward, the sun behind her, casting a golden pathway on the stone floor.

There were burial plaques on the wall, commemorating long-dead Cavalleris. Bryony paused to read them, slowly deciphering the Latin words and numerals. There was the sound of a car in the distance but she was so engrossed that it didn't penetrate her consciousness. Silence fell again, the only sound the buzzing of bees and the call of a distant seabird. Bryony moved on to the next plaque. Suddenly a shadow filled the doorway. Turning quickly, she gave a gasp of fright and shrank back in primitive fear. The figure was so tall, so black and menacing against the brilliant morning light. She saw it was a man, but it was impossible to make out his features with the sun in her eyes. Involuntarily she moved away from him, towards the altar, and said, 'Who — who are you?' in frightened alarm.

The man stepped forward, pushing the door shut behind him with a sharp movement, cutting off the light.

Bryony blinked and could see him now, tall and wide-shouldered, his lean face strong and powerful, his hair dark and thick, and his angry eyes — the eyes that held hers — were like the cold black steel of a sword, and just as dangerous.

He didn't answer her question, instead asked one of his own, his voice like a whiplash. 'What are you doing here? Who allowed you in?'

'The — the door was unlocked.' Immediately she was on the defensive. He took a step towards her and she backed away again, almost tripping over the step that led up to the altar. 'Stay away from me,' she yelled shrilly, fear making her panic.

The man stopped, but his face was still angry. 'Who are you?' He flung her own question back at her.

'I'm staying at the villa. I'm a friend of the Contessa. She knows I'm here,' she added quickly.

His expression changed, became abstracted, cold. 'So she's back.'

The fear was instantly gone. 'You know her? Thank goodness.' Bryony gave a relieved laugh. 'You frightened me. You looked just like——' She broke off. 'Who are *you*?'

His dark glance flicked back to her. 'Who did I look like?'

She shook her head, ashamed of her silly fancy, but he was waiting so she shrugged and said rather ruefully, 'The devil.'

The man's lips twisted in what could have been wry amusement. 'Did I?' His eyes settled on her. 'No, I am not the devil; I am Raphael Cavalleri.' His English was fluent, but she caught the Italian accent now.

'Cavalleri? Then you must be a relation of Etta's?' For a moment he didn't answer, so she said, 'Contessa Henrietta del Cavalleri, the owner of the villa.'

His face hardened as he said tersely, 'I am related to her only by marriage. And she doesn't own this house — I do.'

CHAPTER TWO

'OH, BUT. . .' Bryony had been about to say that he was mistaken, but her words died in her throat; there was something about him that convinced her he wasn't the kind of man to make so important a claim without being able to substantiate it.

'I suppose she told you it was her house,' Raphael Cavalleri said contemptuously.

Disliking his high-handed attitude, Bryony said shortly, 'If you're referring to the Contessa, then the ownership of the house hasn't been mentioned between us.' Which was, strictly speaking, true, although Etta had more than implied that the villa was hers to do as she liked with.

His eyebrows rose at the coldness of her tone and he gave a mocking laugh that put her back up. 'You haven't yet told me who you are,' he reminded her.

Angry herself now, Bryony said challengingly, 'Is it any of your business?'

The challenge was immediately taken up. 'Oh, I think so—if you are staying in my house.'

Bryony gave him a glaring look and went to step past him but he moved to block her way.

'You haven't answered me.'

'My name would mean nothing to you.'

'But I still want to hear it.'

There was no getting past him and he knew it, his eyes holding a hint of triumph as he looked down into her defiant face, her grey eyes full of fierce, helpless anger. Then there was the sound of running footsteps outside and Giovanni arrived in the doorway, out of breath. '*Mi scusi*, I did not——' He broke off in surprise when he saw Bryony. '*Signorina*!'

'*Buon giorno*, Giovanni.' Bryony took the opportunity to step past Raphael Cavalleri and go out of the coolness of the chapel into the sunlight.

But he followed her out and she heard him switch to Italian as he asked Giovanni who she was. 'The *signorina* speaks Italian, *signore*,' Giovanni answered.

Bryony would have liked to see Raphael Cavalleri's face then but she was walking smartly back towards the house and didn't look round, although she heard him say, 'Does she, indeed?' in a surprised tone.

Maria was in the hall, and when Bryony said urgently, 'Where is the Contessa?' immediately led her to a small room off to the right which caught the morning sun and where Etta was having breakfast and working through a pile of letters. She was still in a housecoat but, unlike Bryony, had taken the time to put on her make-up before she came down.

She turned to Bryony with a smile of welcome that quickly faded as she saw her face. 'Why, Bryony, what on earth has upset you?'

'I rather think I have,' Raphael Cavalleri remarked, coming into the room behind her.

'Rafe!' Bryony watched the colour drain from Etta's face, and her hand whiten as it gripped the silver paperknife she was holding. 'What are you doing here?'

'What do you think? Checking on my property, of course. You didn't bother to tell me you were going away.'

'I went to a family wedding.' Etta recovered herself and gave him a look that held both resentment and mockery. 'Aren't you going to say welcome back?'

'I'm sure you will understand if I don't.' He sat down on a chair opposite her without being invited to. 'A cup of coffee, please, Maria,' he said to the maid who was hovering in the doorway.

Maria looked at Etta, who nodded angry permission. 'And the *signorina*? Would you like breakfast?'

It was Bryony's turn to look at Etta, who managed to smile. 'Of course you must have your breakfast, my dear, but it's quite warm this morning so perhaps you would like to have it on the terrace.'

'Of course.'

Bryony took the hint and went to leave but Raphael put out an arm to block her way and said, 'You haven't introduced me to your friend, Etta.' But he looked at Bryony as he spoke, his dark eyes derisive.

She stiffened and Etta looked annoyed, but said, 'Bryony Ferrers; she came back with me from London and is going to stay for a while.'

Raphael inclined his head but there was little politeness in the gesture.

Etta lifted a hand in his direction. 'And this is —— '

But Bryony said shortly, 'Please don't bother. I don't want to know.' And she walked out of the room, feeling that she had retrieved a little of her pride.

Maria brought her coffee and hot rolls out on to the terrace but Bryony had hardly begun to eat before Etta joined her. 'He's gone,' she said thankfully.

'Who on earth is he?' Bryony demanded, completely belying her earlier statement.

'He's Antonio's nephew.'

'He said that *he* owned the villa, not you.'

Etta sighed. 'Well, yes. He inherited the villa and the whole estate when my husband died.'

'You mean he was telling the truth, this is his house?' Bryony gasped.

'Technically, yes. But Antonio left it to me for my lifetime. Rafe can't have it until I die or. . .'

'Or?' Bryony prompted, feeling distinctly uneasy.

'Or I marry again, or leave the house for longer than two months.'

Bryony gave Etta a searching look and then sat back in her chair. 'I think you'd better tell me all about it. It's quite obvious that you and Raphael Cavalleri don't exactly like each other.'

'That is the understatement of the century. We're open enemies. He's hated me ever since Antonio made me his wife and brought me to live here so that he had to leave.'

'You mean he used to live here in the villa?'

'Oh, yes, it's the Cavalleri family home, you see. But Rafe and I didn't get on so I persuaded Antonio to ask him to leave.'

'Well, I can see why your husband had to entail the villa if it's the family home. But why did he make all the conditions for you to keep?'

'Rafe more or less forced him to,' Etta said with a sound very like a snort. 'Oh, he wrapped it up by saying that the future of the villa had to be safeguarded and all that kind of thing. As if I'd do anything terrible to it.'

'But you want to turn it into a hotel,' Bryony pointed out.

'I don't have any choice. I'm quite sure that Antonio also left me the earnings from his estate for my lifetime, but Rafe won't hand them over. He says they weren't included. Of course, I'm trying to get them through my lawyer, but there are so many layers of bureaucracy on this island, and not being a native Italian. . .' Etta shrugged eloquently. 'Even if I do succeed it could take years. And in the meantime I have to live and to maintain this house.'

'But surely your husband left you enough to——' Bryony broke off. 'I'm sorry, it's none of my business.'

'Oh, I don't mind. Actually it's nice to have someone

to talk it over with. Antonio did provide for me, of course. He invested a huge sum for me when we got married and I live off the income from that, but it isn't enough to maintain the house as well.' A vengeful look came into her eyes. 'It's all Rafe's doing. He wants me out. And he hopes that by depriving me of money he'll make sure that I'll have to give up the house to him and go back to England.'

Trying to ignore her initial meeting with Rafe and see it from both sides, Bryony said, 'Well, I suppose he must have resented being turned out of his home and not being able to come back to it when his uncle died as he expected. Was he brought up here?' And when Etta nodded, 'Well, maybe he wants to bring his family up here, too.'

'He has no family. He isn't married.'

'Really?' Bryony was surprised. 'I thought he would have been. He must be about thirty, mustn't he?'

'He's thirty-two. But I don't find it at all surprising. He isn't the type to get married. He's the kind of man you have for a lover. Until he tires of you and leaves you for someone new.'

She spoke vehemently and it suddenly occurred to Bryony to wonder just why Etta and Rafe hadn't got on. Had he made a pass at her that had been rejected — or perhaps even the other way round?

But the thought was pushed to the back of her mind when Etta leaned forward and touched her hand, saying, 'You didn't like him either, did you? What did he say to you?'

Bryony shrugged. 'It wasn't what he said so much as his attitude. He behaved as if I were an intruder; he wasn't even polite.'

'That's typical. Coming here and acting as if he owned the place. Ordering my staff about as if I had no right to be here. He takes every opportunity to humiliate me and try to drive me out.'

Looking at her with sympathy, Bryony said, 'Wouldn't it be easier for you to give up the villa and go back to England if he's making your life so unpleasant?'

'Give in to him?' A martial light came into Etta's eyes. 'Never! I'd stay on here just to spite him even if I didn't love the place. But I do; Antonio and I were happy here. And why the hell should I leave? Antonio left it to me, and, as that was about all he did leave me, then I'm going to hang on to it and not be pushed out by that arrogant trickster!'

Bryony burst out laughing and clapped her hands. 'Good for you! I'm behind you all the way. As far as I'm concerned men are the pits.'

Etta grinned. 'I'm not quite sure what that expression means, but I entirely agree.'

They looked at each other and laughed. Then Bryony's face sobered as she said, 'But what about your plans for turning the villa into a hotel? Surely Rafe won't allow you to?'

'You didn't tell him about the project, did you?' Etta asked with an anxious look.

'No, of course not.'

'That was lucky. Rafe was one of the things I was going to tell you about,' Etta added.

'Perhaps before we'd left England might have been a good time,' Bryony pointed out wryly.

'But then you might not have come,' Etta said sagely. 'And I need you, Bryony, I really do. I'm determined to get this hotel project off the ground.'

'But will Rafe let you?' Bryony asked again.

'He can't stop me. I've had two lawyers go over Antonio's will and there's nothing to stop me using the house as I wish.'

'But don't you have to get permission from the planning authorities for change of use?'

Etta smiled thinly. 'Bureaucracy works both ways, remember.'

'But surely if Rafe has influence. . .'

'Yes, but he won't want any scandal attached to the family name. I do have that hold over him. I can threaten to create such a fuss that he'll find it very difficult to use any but open, legal channels. But I don't want him to know anything about our plans until the place is established.' She reached over to cover Bryony's hand again. 'Will you help me, Bryony, dear? I suppose I should have told you all this before you came, but I so badly needed someone like yourself to help me and give me moral support. And you being able to speak Italian is such an asset. Will you stay? Please?'

Always a sucker for a sob story, Bryony probably would have said yes anyway, but, having met Rafe Cavalleri and seen how arrogantly he behaved, she had no hesitation in saying, 'Of course I will. And don't worry; I won't let him drive you out.' Which was a supremely optimistic promise considering the way Rafe had almost held her against her will in the chapel earlier. And purely by the force of his dominant personality, too. Bryony felt an inward shiver, wondering just what she was taking on, and whether turning Rafe into an enemy wasn't an extremely stupid idea. But Etta certainly needed help, and she was committed now. And a problematic future would, she thought cynically, certainly take her mind off the recent past.

They pushed Rafe out of their minds; Etta went up to dress and then showed Bryony round the villa. Besides the rooms that Bryony had seen, there was a huge dining-room with a very long central table, a library, and a large morning-room, all of them furnished in the same rich taste. She and Etta worked out that they would have enough rooms in the house for twelve guests, and there were another two rooms in the tower that could be made into a suite if the bathroom between the rooms could be improved. 'Antonio and I did a lot of entertaining,' Etta explained. 'That's why the bedrooms in the villa all have *en-suite* bathrooms, but we never had more than twelve guests to stay at the most, so there was no need to update the tower.'

'What about the dining-room?' Bryony questioned. 'Are all the guests to eat at the big table?'

'Oh, I think so, don't you? That way they'll feel more as if they're guests than paying customers. That's how I want them to feel.'

'Fine, but what if we only have a few guests to start with? They'll be lost round that table.'

'Then we'll use the small one. And we can also use that at breakfast-time for people who don't want to eat on the terrace.'

'All right. How much are you thinking of charging, by the way?' Etta stated a sum in hundreds of thousands of lira, and Bryony, after having translated it into English pounds, said, 'That would be for a week?'

Etta looked shocked. 'No, dear, for a night. We want to keep the hotel exclusive.'

'At that price it certainly will be,' Bryony returned. 'I doubt if there's anyone who could afford it.'

'No, you're wrong,' Etta said with certainty. 'I travelled a lot when I was married to Antonio and we stayed at a great many hotels like this will be, and believe me there are plenty of people who are willing to pay for the best, for the privilege of staying in what is virtually a private home.'

'Well, I'll take your word for it; it's out of my league. What about staff—you can't expect Giovanni and Maria to look after a hotel full of guests?'

'Of course not, but I can hire help locally to clean and make beds and that kind of thing; I always did that when we entertained. And Maria can help you prepare the food and then help Giovanni to serve it. I think we'll have to play it by ear, hiring staff as and when we need them.'

'Sounds good. When do you plan to open?'

'As soon as possible. I'll phone round all my friends and let them know and ask them to pass the word on.'

'Won't they resent having to pay—your friends?' Bryony queried, foreseeing difficulties.

'No, dear, they all know how badly I've been treated and that I've been driven to this.'

'Fine.' Bryony looked at Etta. 'So all we have to do is give the place a name.'

'I've been thinking about that,' Etta smiled. 'How about the Hotel Giorgione?' explaining when Bryony frowned in puzzlement, 'He was an Italian painter—a great rival of the artist Raphael's, so I understand.'

Bryony burst out laughing. 'Etta, you're incorrigible.'

That evening Bryony grabbed the phone long enough to tell her parents that she'd arrived safely, then Etta took over to run up an astronomical bill as she phoned various friends all over the world. Leaving her to it, Bryony went down to the kitchen, which she was relieved to find fitted with all the cookers, working surfaces, and every modern gadget she might need. 'When the Conte and Contessa entertained we had a chef who came from Palermo to do the cooking,' Maria explained. 'For him everything had to be just so.'

'And for me,' Bryony said firmly. 'I, too, am a chef.'

She stayed in the kitchen, talking to them in Italian, although their English was almost fluent from having worked for Etta for so long, but Bryony wanted to establish a good relationship with them if they were all to work together. And she wanted to let them know from the start that her standards were as high as any chef from Palermo. After arranging to go shopping with Maria the next morning so that she could see what produce was on offer at the local markets, Bryony went upstairs to join Etta again and work out what they would need in the way of linen and that kind of thing for the rooms. But Etta and her late husband had entertained so much that there was little to be bought.

'Except stationery and ledgers; we will need to buy some of those.'

They began to work out what they would need when the phone rang and Etta went to answer it, greeting the caller as a friend. When she put the receiver down she came over and gave Bryony a hug. 'That was an American contact. He's bringing over a group of six for two weeks—and they'll be arriving a week on Saturday! Isn't that marvellous?'

'Great!' Bryony enthused. She lifted a glowing face to Etta. 'So we're in business.'

Maria didn't drive, so the next morning Giovanni drove them in a rather battered estate car down to the nearest town, dropping the two women off while he went on to the stationer's. Walking round the markets, Bryony found them a cornucopia of fresh fruits and vegetables, and the surrounding sea provided an immense variety of fish and shellfish. For an hour or so Maria went round with her, explaining what all the things that were strange to Bryony were used for, but then she went off to do some shopping of her own and Bryony, finding the sunny weather pleasantly warm even if the Sicilians didn't, sat at a table outside a café and ordered a coffee.

The café was on a corner, where the cars and people coming from the town had to stop and wait at an intersection to cross, the cars heading for the main highway, the people for the car park and bus station. It was fun watching the busy scene; the island seemed to be well-populated and nearly everyone had cars from the way they filled the streets. In turn, her fair hair, this morning drawn up into a plait that started on top of her head and reached her shoulders, caught the attention of many passers-by. Not only pedestrians; several car drivers hooted as they waited for the lights to change or swept past. Bryony ignored them, but it wasn't so easy to ignore a young man who walked past giving her a long look, loitered on the corner for a while to see if she was alone, then came back.

''Allo, miss,' the youth said, putting a hand on the chair next to hers. 'I sit with you?' Before Bryony could reply he had pulled out a chair and sat down. 'You very pretty, miss,' he told her, giving her his best smile.

Bryony looked at him contemplatively. It had been a long time since she had been picked up and she wasn't quite sure that she still knew how to handle it. To bluntly tell him to get lost would have been easy, of course, but he looked pleasant enough, his smile was attractive in a quite handsome face and he was clean and quite smartly dressed. She decided to give him a gentle brush-off instead.

'I buy you a drink?' he offered.

Shaking her head, Bryony pointed to her still half-full coffee-cup. 'No, thank you. How did you know I was English?'

Clearly pleased that she had spoken to him, he said, 'You have beautiful blonde hair. And your face——' he went to touch her cheek but Bryony moved away '—has no tan.'

'I see.'

'My name is Alessandro,' the young man told her. 'You are here on holiday, pretty miss? I show you Sicily. I have a car. I can give you very good time.'

'Thank you, but I'm not on holiday.'

'No?' He looked uncertain.

'No.' She shook her head, then, looking into his long-lashed brown eyes, relented a little. 'I am here to work. I have a job.'

'You work in Sicily?' He stared at her. 'Only English girls who are couriers work in Sicily. And they speak Italian.' He drew back a little. 'You speak Italian?'

Bryony nodded, looking at him impishly.

He shook his head at her. 'You play with me, pretty miss.'

She laughed, but said placatingly, 'But your English is so good.'

'No, not good.' An idea came to him and he leaned forward eagerly. 'You teach me English, yes?'

Before she could reply, Bryony's attention was caught by the sound of a car braking sharply, those behind it hooting angrily as they, too, stood on their brakes. Glancing up, she saw that a silver-coloured sports car had stopped at the junction although the lights were green. At the wheel was the one man in the whole of Sicily whom she recognised. It was Raphael Cavalleri, and he was glaring at her with the blackest frown she'd ever seen.

Held still by surprise, Bryony gazed back until he put the car into gear and accelerated away. Watching her, Alessandro said, 'You know that man?'

'What?' It occurred to Bryony that she had the perfect way to get rid of him. 'Oh, yes. He is a friend, a great friend,' she added expressively.

'Him? He is your—your friend?' Alessandro looked stunned.

'Do you know him?'

He threw wide his arms in an encompassing gesture. 'Everyone in the town, in Sicily, knows that car.' He got quickly to his feet. 'It was good to meet you, pretty miss.'

She laughed. 'Don't you want to learn English any more?'

He grinned back. 'I find a pretty miss with no friend.' And he gave her a sweeping wave of his hand as he walked away, trying to swagger and look nonchalant, but walking briskly for all that.

Glancing at her watch, Bryony saw that she still had another twenty minutes to wait before she met Maria. There were some really delicious-looking cakes in the display stand in the café window. Bryony had resisted them before but now she ordered one with another cup of coffee. Taking a notebook from her bag, she began to work out some menus that would incorporate the produce she had seen in the market. Someone stopped in front of her and didn't move on. Another pick-up, she thought resignedly, seeing a pair of trousered legs, and determinedly kept her head down.

'Miss Ferrers?'

'Signor Cavalleri.' Reluctantly she looked up and greeted him formally, without a smile. Rafe hadn't wasted any time parking his car and getting here; it was less than ten minutes since he'd passed.

'Your friend has gone?'

'As you see.'

He, too, sat down beside her, but unlike Alessandro he didn't even bother to ask her permission. As yesterday, he was wearing a dark business suit. The café proprietor, obviously recognising him, came dashing out to take his order, whereas Bryony had had to go inside to the counter. When the man had gone Rafe turned to her and said, 'I thought that you had arrived in Sicily only two days ago?'

'Yes, I did,' Bryony replied, adding pointedly, 'Good morning. How are you?'

His brows flickered and Rafe lifted his chin a little, aware that she was teaching him a lesson. 'Good morning. I am well, thank you. And you?' he asked in a voice heavy with irony.

'Fine. How strange that you should be passing.'

'Not really. All the traffic leaving the town has to pass this way.'

'But how strange that, having driven by, you should find it necessary to walk back again,' and she raised her eyes to meet his with an innocent look.

But she had met her match. Rafe merely said, 'Isn't it?' in a tone as bland as her own. His coffee arrived and as he stirred it he said, 'Have you stayed with Etta before?'

'No, this is my first visit.'

'But you know her well?'

Aware that he must be curious about her and even more about her connection with Etta, Bryony said merely, 'Well enough.'

'But you never met my uncle, Antonio?'

'No.'

'So you can't have known Etta long, then; my uncle died less than a year ago.'

'But I don't suppose they went everywhere together, did they? Although they were very close, of course,' she added, pushing Etta's claim.

'Just where did you meet Etta?' Rafe demanded bluntly.

It was difficult to avoid such a straight question but Bryony did her best. 'In England. Why don't you try one of these cakes? They're delicious.'

But he ignored the diversion. 'Where in England?'

'At a party.'

'A party? His voice sharpened. 'Not the family wedding she said she went to?'

'Good heavens, no. That was only a week ago,' Bryony said airily.

'But you know about it.'

'Yes, of course. I was there.'

Rafe immediately pounced on her. 'At a family wedding?'

Cursing inwardly, Bryony said, 'Etta and I do have a — family connection.'

'Do you, indeed? What connection is that exactly?'

But Bryony bit into her cake. 'These pastries are really good. Are all the cakes on Sicily as good as this?'

'Definitely. You have cream on your upper lip.' And he watched her as she put out the tip of her tongue to lick it off. 'Haven't you been to Sicily before?'

'No, this is my first time.'

Rafe's eyebrows rose above dark eyes that held a taunting glint. 'Really? Then you must make friends very quickly.'

'Oh, no, I don't know anyone here — except you, of course, and I would hardly describe you as a friend.'

'Wouldn't you? Then how would you describe the young man you were with earlier?'

Annoyed at falling into his trap, Bryony didn't make it worse by letting it embarrass her. 'I wasn't with him. He was trying to pick me up,' she admitted calmly.

His face hardening, Rafe said acidly, 'And you allow that?'

'If I'd allowed it he would still be here,' she pointed out.

'But you were talking to him.'

Bryony finished her cake and drained her cup of coffee. 'Why not? *He* wasn't offensive.' And she laid a definite stress on the pronoun.

'You let strange men speak to you, pick you up?'

'I've already told you he didn't. I got rid of him.' Tilting her head, she gave him an enigmatic smile. 'It was very easy, really — getting rid of him.'

Her tone invited his question and Rafe knew it; he

paused for a long moment before complying. 'So how did you get rid of him?'

Bryony got to her feet and looked down at him, her gaze sardonic. 'He recognised your car, so I let him think that *you* were my lover.' She smiled sweetly as his eyes widened in astonishment. 'Goodbye, Signor Cavalleri.' And she strode away.

But she hadn't gone three yards before he caught her up and, grabbing her arm, swung her round to face him. Bryony had been feeling quite triumphant but one look at the blazing anger in his eyes brought her rapidly down to earth. 'I suppose you think that was very funny,' he said savagely. 'Before long it will be all over the island.'

'Too bad,' Bryony retorted, trying to defy him.

'Really? And how will you like it then, being pointed out as my mistress? Or doesn't that matter to you?' Rafe added malevolently, 'If you can speak to strangers on the street so easily then maybe you don't care what you're thought of.'

Her cheeks paled a little, but Bryony shrugged and said, 'He doesn't know who I am.'

Rafe gave short, mirthless laugh. 'Not at the moment, perhaps, but it would be easy for him to find out—especially if I saw that the rumour was spread. And it definitely wouldn't help Etta's standing on this island if everyone knew she had a woman of—that type, staying with her, would it?'

Bryony's head came up as she faced him defiantly. 'Are you threatening me?'

For a second surprise showed in his dark eyes, but then Rafe shrugged in a very Latin gesture. 'If you like to think so.'

Refusing to be intimidated, Bryony remembered her conversation about him when Etta had said that he wouldn't like any scandal, so she said, 'OK, go ahead

and spread your rumours if that's the kind of man you
are, but don't forget that *you'll* be gossiped about as
well. And all for nothing,' she added pertly. 'And now
I really must be going — I have another man to meet.'
She glanced over his shoulder. 'By the way, the café
proprietor is watching you. Hadn't you better go and
pay your bill? Wouldn't want to be arrested, now,
would you?' And this time she did manage to walk
away as he swung round to look behind him.

When they got back to the villa Bryony thought it
wiser not to say anything to Etta about her encounter
with Rafe. They had lunch and then Etta went upstairs,
to write some letters, she said, although Bryony had a
strong suspicion it was to take a siesta. At a loose end,
Bryony walked down through the garden, past the
tennis court, and on down through a sloping orchard of
orange and lemon trees. And beyond them she came to
a path that led down through rocky crags to a small
beach and the sea.

Taking off her shoes, Bryony ran on to the sand,
enjoying the soft feel of it between her bare toes. There
were rocks stretching out into the sea at either side of
the beach, giving it a feeling of privacy. Perhaps it
belonged to the villa. How marvellous to have your
own private beach, she thought, and wondered why
Etta hadn't mentioned it. There was a wooden jetty,
too, not in the best repair, with part of its edge washed
away by the sea. She looked round, thinking that the
beach would certainly be a great asset to the hotel. And
the sand was beautifully soft and clean, with only a drift
of seaweed at the waterline. The water was cold as she
waded in a little way, but she walked along to her right,
enjoying herself, and stooping to pick up a pretty
seashell.

Coming to the jetty, she climbed the steps and
walked along its length, finding big metal rings ham-

mered into the uprights. So boats must come in here, then, or had in the past. It reminded her that Sicily was, and had always been, an island with strong seafaring links all over the Mediterranean. The thought conjured up pictures of pirates and slave ships, of greed and cruelty. Bryony shivered suddenly, as if someone had walked over her grave, and turned to go back to the beach, feeling glad of the sun's warmth. Above her seagulls wheeled and dived, their cries raucous, like screams. The sea was capped with white-crested waves and became grey and unwelcoming as a large dark cloud obscured the sun. The beach no longer seemed such a peaceful haven, and Bryony hurried back to the path, putting on her shoes, and running back to the villa.

That evening she took over the kitchen, giving Maria and Giovanni a night off, and experimented with some of the produce she'd bought in the market, writing the menu on a card embossed with the Cavalleri family crest. Etta smiled delightedly when she saw it. 'You've written it out so beautifully!' she exclaimed. 'It looks really professional.'

'Calligraphy was one of the courses I took when I was living with Jeff and had nothing else to do,' Bryony explained. 'I'm glad you're pleased. As a matter of fact, I was wondering whether it might be possible to give your guests a copy of the dinner menu every day to keep as a souvenir.'

'Of course, that's a marvellous idea,' Etta enthused. 'A nice touch but one that wouldn't cost too much, except for your time in writing them out, of course. Would it take you very long?'

'No, I can do it quickly.' She tapped the menu card with her finger. 'But it's the crest that makes it look so imposing, of course.'

'Yes.' Etta gave the two heraldic beasts, a wyvern

holding a sword and above it an eagle with spread wings, a reflective look. 'Don't you think they look rather overpowering for a hotel? Maybe we ought to have a gentler emblem.'

'You mean something like a chef, rampant, holding a rolling-pin?' Bryony laughed. 'I think the customers would prefer the original. And, after all, it is your coat of arms.'

'No, not really mine; it was Antonio's — and the rest of the Cavalleri family,' Etta said meaningfully.

'Ah, I understand. You mean that Rafe wouldn't like it.'

'Quite.'

'If you're not going to tell him about the hotel, then he's hardly likely to find out.'

Etta sighed. 'I'd like to think that was so, but he always seems to find out everything sooner or later. Look at the way he found out that I'd gone to England. I certainly didn't let him know.'

After hesitating a moment Bryony said, 'Maria and Giovanni; do you think they might have —— ?'

'Oh, no!' Etta said at once. 'They are a hundred per cent loyal to me. They were working for an American friend of mine who had a flat in Rome, but she died, and they were out of a home and a job. So I took over the flat and they worked for me for a couple of years before I married Antonio, and then they came here with me. It worked out beautifully because Antonio's old housekeeper was ready to retire anyway.' She laughed. 'In fact, I think Antonio married me as much for Maria and Giovanni as he did for myself.'

'Well, if it isn't them,' Bryony said, bringing her back to the subject, 'then who?'

'It could be anyone around here. The gardener has been here a long time so he knew Rafe when he lived here, of course. And he lives in the village and probably gossips to his neighbours, so Rafe could find out that way.'

'He's bound to find out about the hotel, then.'

'Eventually, I suppose, but I've told Maria and Giovanni not to say anything, and as far as the rest of the staff will know the customers will be just my guests. We'll keep paying the bills discreet,' she added with a conspiratorial wink.

But this time Bryony didn't laugh. 'I imagine that Rafe could make things very difficult and unpleasant if he wanted to.'

Etta nodded reluctantly. 'He tried to buy me out when Antonio died. He wanted me to take the money he offered me and give up the villa to him. And when I wouldn't he said I would regret it.' She lifted a hand expressively. 'It was a threat, of course, but he didn't shout or anything, he just said it in that icily cold voice of his.' She shuddered theatrically. 'I felt quite frightened. That's why I'm so glad you're here,' Etta added. 'I feel so much more confident and — and safe now.'

Bryony smiled, but when she went up to her room that night and stood at the window, looking out at the moonlight before closing the curtains, she thought that Etta's confidence was entirely misplaced. She was no barrier against Rafe Cavalleri's malevolence. In fact she had probably made it worse by taking that cheap rise out of him in the town this morning. But it was his fault; she wouldn't have done it if Rafe hadn't glowered at her so angrily from his car. Well, it was too late now, and Bryony couldn't be altogether sorry; it had given her quite a lift to show him that she couldn't be intimidated so easily.

But now, she thought, pulling the curtain across, it might be a much better idea to keep well away from Rafe in future.

The next day Etta hired a couple of young men from

the village to come and work on the overgrown garden
and to clean out the swimming-pool, which hadn't been
used since the previous summer. She and Bryony were
busy for the next couple of days in turning a small room
on the ground floor that Antonio had used as a study
into an office, and in working out an accounting and
filing system. For all her airiness, Etta turned out to
have a good basic business sense, and she hadn't
plucked the amount they were going to charge out of
thin air, she had worked out the probable overheads
and added a hefty profit margin. Bryony was amused to
see her own salary included.

'There will be times when we won't have any guests,'
Etta remarked. 'Until word gets around, of course.'

'Have you thought of having dinner parties for small
groups from other hotels? I'm sure people will be eager
to meet a real live *contessa*, especially if the cooking
and the ambience are good. Then they might want to
come and stay here, or will at least tell their friends.'

'Oh, I like that idea,' Etta said enthusiastically. 'We'd
have to dress it up, of course. Make it a big occasion,
so they'll remember and tell all their friends. But what
if they don't speak English? You'd have to act as
interpreter. But you can't do that if you're in the
kitchen.'

'I'm sure we'll be able to work something out,'
Bryony said soothingly. 'Would you like me to put
together some sample menus so that we can figure out
what to charge? Oh, and we'll need wines of course.
We haven't talked about that yet. Do you know a good
supplier?'

'I have an excellent supplier — and a very convenient
one, too.' Etta stood up and beckoned Bryony to follow
her.

They went across the hall to the kitchen and through

a door that led to a cellar, its stone walls surprisingly evenly hewn, the ceiling vaulted.

'There used to be a much older house here,' Etta told her. 'But this is all that's left. So Antonio stored his wine here.' And she gestured towards the receding racks that filled the long, wide room down its middle and left-hand side. On the right-hand wall there was a long line of barrels on their sides, resting on strong wooden trestles. 'Those are the sherries and Madeira,' Etta told her. 'Enough for you?'

'More than enough,' Bryony agreed in astonishment. 'An army could get drunk down here. Have you got a record of everything?'

'Antonio made one. He took a great pride in his cellar. But I'm afraid I haven't bothered much since he died. Giovanni just comes and gets a bottle as we need it.'

'Perhaps it would be a good idea if I went through his list and updated it,' Bryony offered.

'Wonderful. Antonio kept it in that safe in his study, so it must still be there.'

They began to walk along the racks, looking at the labels, but Giovanni came to the head of the stairs and called down to them. 'There is a telephone call.'

'I'll come up,' Etta replied.

'No, Contessa, it is for Signorina Ferrers,' he told them, pronouncing Bryony's surname with some difficulty. 'A man.'

'It must be my father. Oh, I hope nothing's happened to any of my grandparents.'

She ran upstairs and hurried to the phone, ignoring Giovanni when he tried to speak to her. Grabbing up the receiver, she said anxiously, 'Hello? What's happened?'

'*Signorina*. . .' The voice that answered was far dif-

ferent from that of her father's and his accent sounded
stronger over the phone. 'This is Raphael Cavalleri.'

'Oh.' Bryony could find nothing else to say.

'Hello. How are you?' he said sardonically mimicking
her own irony of a couple of days before.

'Very well, thank you. I was surprised to receive a
call from you. I expected it to be someone else.'

'Oh, who?'

'No one you know,' she answered repressively. 'Why
have you rung me?'

'It occurred to me that as this is your first visit to
Sicily you won't have seen Taormina yet. I wondered if
you would care to drive up there with me and have
dinner after looking at the town?'

'What?' Bryony was completely taken aback.

'I said——'

'No, I heard you. I just—couldn't believe what I was
hearing.'

'Does it surprise you so much?'

'Yes, it does,' she said bluntly.

'But you're a very attractive girl; why shouldn't I
want to take you out?'

Bryony could think of a hundred reasons, but merely
said, 'We aren't exactly on sociable terms.'

'That can be remedied,' Rafe replied, far too
smoothly for her liking. 'And, after all, if the rumour
you started is going to be spread about, then we may as
well give it some substance, don't you think?'

'Now that I believe,' Bryony said shortly. 'Sorry, I'm
not in the mood for fuelling your ego tonight. Goodbye.' And she put the phone down.

Her face flushed, she went to join Etta in the sitting-
room.

'It wasn't bad news, was it?' Etta asked, trying to
keep the anxiety out of her voice as she looked
searchingly at the younger woman.

'What?'

'About your grandparents?'

'Oh. No. It wasn't Daddy.' She put her hands on her hips. 'It was Rafe.'

'Rafe!' Etta's eyes widened. 'Why was he calling *you*?'

'To ask me out to dinner, no less. In Taormina.'

Etta's eyes opened even wider. 'He did? But why should he. . .?' She tried to work it out. 'He must be trying to get at me through you in some way. What did you say?'

'No, of course. But I don't think it's you he wants to get at.' Briefly she told Etta about her meeting with him in the town.

'You did what?' Etta gazed at her open-mouthed while Bryony waited for her anger. But then Etta burst into peals of laughter. 'Oh, I love it! He must have been furious.' Then she sobered. 'I think we both have him for an enemy now. But what the hell?' She shrugged. 'At least we can fight him together.'

They talked for a while longer and then Etta went out to a cocktail party. It was too early to eat, so Bryony went down into the cellar to get the wine record up to date. It was dusty and cool down there so she was wearing jeans and a loose sweater, her hair pulled back off her head. She had been down there for nearly an hour and was halfway along the racks when she heard the cellar door open and male footsteps coming down.

'I'm over here, Giovanni,' she called out.

The footsteps came nearer, but it was Rafe who came to the end of the rack and stood there, a couple of glasses in his hand.

Bryony was so surprised that she nearly dropped the bottle she was holding. Quickly he put out his free hand and caught it. 'Lucky you didn't break it,' he said, looking at the label. 'That's a good year.'

'Must you keep appearing out of nowhere like — like some demon?' she said angrily.

'You left me no choice,' he said. And bent down and kissed her.

CHAPTER THREE

THE sound of the slap echoed round the cellar. Lifting his hand, Rafe rubbed the back of it against his cheek. He didn't look hurt or even angry, just surprised. 'No one has ever done that to me before.'

'You amaze me,' Bryony said acidly.

'And you me,' he answered, an amused look coming into his eyes.

The amusement disconcerted her; she'd expected him to be furious with her for hitting him, for wounding his dignity as much as for rejecting his kiss so violently. Her grey eyes flashing fire, she said, 'If that was what you came for then you can get out.'

Rafe gave her a contemplative look. 'But I had to come; you gave me no choice.'

'What are you talking about?'

'You refused to have dinner with me,' he reminded her. 'So I decided to join you here at the villa.'

'Had you thought of waiting until you were invited?' she asked sarcastically.

'Yes, but I thought I might have to wait some time, so I invited myself instead.'

His cool high-handedness took her aback for a moment, but then Bryony said, 'I hardly think that you and Etta will——'

'Ah, but Etta is not here. And I happen to know that she will be joining some friends for dinner after the cocktail party she's attending.' He didn't add that they would therefore be alone, deliberately, Bryony thought, and couldn't understand why. But he was right about Etta; his spy system was working well for him.

He held up the glasses. 'Giovanni said you were in the cellar so I thought it would be an idea to have an aperitif down here. There's plenty to choose from.' He looked round the vaulted room and walked over to the other side where the barrels were stored. 'Do you like your sherry sweet or dry?'

Bryony watched him for a moment, puzzled by his attitude. 'What makes you think I want to drink with you, let alone have dinner?'

'You would rather eat alone?' he asked without turning round.

Would she? Bryony hesitated for a fraction of a second too long before saying, 'I'm not bored by my own company.'

'You wouldn't be bored with mine,' he answered, turning to face her.

There was something about him at that moment, as he stood with his athletic body and leanly handsome face outlined by the harsh lights of the cellar, that caught at Bryony's emotions. She hadn't really looked at him as a man before, just as someone who had been overbearing and rude. But now she saw how masculinely attractive he was, and guessed that he could be charming, given the right woman. But she definitely wasn't the right woman. And if he turned the charm on to her it would only be to suit his own ends. Ends that she couldn't at the moment fathom.

His mouth quirking a little, as if he could read her thoughts, Rafe said, 'You haven't answered my question. I asked you what kind of sherry you like.'

'Medium.'

He nodded, carefully keeping any satisfaction out of his face, and went over to fill the glasses from one of the larger barrels. Lifting one of the delicate crystal glasses, he held it to the light, looking at the rich amber colour of the liquid, then held it out to her. 'Try this.'

She took the glass and sipped. 'It's very good. One of the best I've tasted.'

'My uncle laid it down some years ago. *Salute*!' He clinked his own glass against hers, gently, no more than a touch, but his eyes, dark and penetrating, held her gaze until Bryony blinked and looked quickly away.

There was a fleeting look of satisfaction in his eyes, but then Rafe stepped away from her and, picking up the wine-record book, flipped through the pages.

'I see you're bringing it up to date. Did Etta ask you to?'

'No, I offered.'

She didn't enlarge on it and he said, 'You've started on the French vintages. Are you a connoisseur?'

Bryony was, in that she had taken several courses in wine at the cordon bleu school, and also later to increase her experience and growing interest, but she thought it better not to tell him that, so she said, 'They were nearest the door.'

'Ah, of course.' He put the book down. 'Will you be staying in Sicily long?'

Another leading question which she wasn't prepared to answer. Talking to him was like walking through a minefield. 'How long is long?' she countered.

His eyes went quickly to her face. 'Most people who come here on holiday stay for two or three weeks only.'

'Hardly enough time to see the island properly, I should have thought.'

'No, but that is usually all the time they have.'

'Yes, I suppose so.' Turning, she went towards the cellar steps. 'I'll finish this job some other time. Shall we go up?' And, neatly avoiding having to answer his question, she began to climb the stairs without bothering to wait for him.

Giovanni was hovering in the hall. 'I'm sorry, *signorina*. I could not stop him.'

'It's all right, Giovanni.'

He looked at her uncertainly. 'Maria and I, we were going to the town, but if you wish we will stay. . .' His voice trailed off as he saw Rafe follow her up from the cellar, carrying a bottle of wine.

Bryony hesitated. She didn't want to be left alone with Rafe, wasn't sure she could handle him if he tried anything again. But she didn't see why everyone should have their plans upset by him. 'Then you must go,' she said with a smile. 'Signor Cavalleri is just leaving,' she added firmly, turning to face Rafe determinedly.

'Am I? I thought we were having dinner together.'

'No, we're not.'

'It would be a shame not to drink this wine. It's a very good vintage.'

'Then I'll drink it alone.'

Tilting his head a little to one side, Rafe gave her an appealing look. 'Not even if I promise to behave like a perfect gentleman? Do I have that phrase right?'

'Yes, you have the phrase right, but not the description — you are *not* a gentleman.'

His head came up at that and for a moment his face hardened, but then he shrugged. 'Perhaps I deserved that.' He set the bottle down on the big oval table and, coming up to her, took her hand. 'You have dust on your cheek.' Using the back of his finger, he gently brushed it off, an expression in his eyes she hadn't seen there before. Then he gave a small bow. 'Very well, *signorina*, I will leave you to your solitary meal. *Buon appetito*.' And, lifting her hand to his mouth, he kissed it, his eyes on her face before he turned quickly and strode to the door which Giovanni had opened for him.

Bryony thought that he would just go, but on the threshold he paused, and seemed almost reluctantly to look back and lift his hand in salute. '*Arrivederci*, Bryony.'

Was that a casual goodbye or a threat? Bryony didn't know and she didn't answer. When the heavy door had closed behind him, she went round the house with Giovanni, making sure all the other doors were locked, the windows closed. Shortly afterwards he and Maria left and Bryony took her tray of food into the small sitting-room where the television set was the central feature. She began to eat, but after a few moments went into the hall and picked up the bottle of wine that Rafe had chosen. It was very good, like nectar to the palate. If nothing else he knew his wines.

But he was far more than just a wine buff, Bryony was sure of that. He was like an iceberg with most of his personality hidden deep away, or a diamond that showed only one, or perhaps two, of its facets. Because Rafe had been different today—after she'd slapped his face, of course. Bryony wondered uneasily just what had prompted him to kiss her. Had it been a spur-of-the-moment impulse, or had he come to the villa with the express intention of trying to seduce her? When he'd seen her in the town with Alessandro, the boy who'd tried to pick her up, Rafe had accused her of being cheap. Maybe he had decided to try his luck, although he didn't seem to be the type who would want or need casual sex. No, if it was deliberate then he had some deeper motive in mind, Bryony decided. And the only motive he could have would be to harm Etta in some way.

Her meal finished, Bryony refilled her glass, turned off the television set that she hadn't been watching anyway, and walked through to the main sitting-room where she let herself out of the French windows on to the terrace. Leaning on the rail, she savoured the stillness of the night. It was a beautiful evening, the moon silvering the trees and bushes in the garden, and casting deep shadows where the old walls separating

the garden from the driveway rose high against the sky.
Scents, unusual to her English nose, drifted on the
breeze. Tomorrow, she thought, I'll go round the
garden and smell every flower, find out which ones the
scents come from. In the distance the sea shimmered in
the moonlight, always moving, like a living thing.

It was all very beautiful, worth fighting for. As Rafe
Cavalleri was fighting for it, in his own way, she
supposed. It must have been a blow to him when his
uncle got married so late in life and then left the house
to his widow. Especially as he had been brought up here
and looked on it as his home. Etta had a right to be afraid
of him. Not that Etta had mentioned any physical fear
of Rafe, only of his driving her out of the house.

Almost reluctantly Bryony dragged her mind back to
her own part in this. She was hardly of the age-group
for Etta to invite her as an ordinary house guest, so
Rafe must, she knew, be intensely curious about her.
And annoyed that he could find nothing out because
his spies in the village knew nothing. So perhaps he had
decided to try to find out for himself by asking her to
have dinner with him. It just showed the arrogance of
the man if he thought she would accept after the way
he'd behaved to her, Bryony thought scornfully. He
must think he's God's gift to women! But didn't most
men, deep down, think that? Especially Latins, who
had been spoiled rotten by their womenfolk for
centuries. And Rafe was certainly good-looking enough
to have won over scores of women, so why shouldn't
he think he could do the same with her? After all, he
already thought of her as cheap.

Her cheeks flushed with anger, Bryony forced herself
to concentrate. OK, so that was why he had kissed her,
she decided firmly. But would he really stoop so low
just to find out who she was? She doubted it. He
probably had something far more devious in mind. For

her to spy on Etta for him, most likely. He couldn't suborn Giovanni and Maria, so he would use her instead. The worm! Bryony took a deep drink, remembering the sudden flare of attraction she'd felt for him. Thank heavens she'd sent him packing. Under the influence of this bottle of wine and his charm, who knew what she might have let slip to Rafe? The last thing she wanted to do was to harm Etta or her project in any way. But at least she now knew why Rafe had come here tonight, why he'd kissed her with lips that for a brief moment had lit a flame of longing inside her.

He was so devious! So devious, in fact, that she wouldn't be surprised if Rafe hadn't had even deeper reasons for what he'd done — or tried to do. She tried hard to concentrate. Perhaps he —

'Bryony? Are you out there?'

Her thoughts were shattered as Etta called to her from the sitting-room. Bryony went quickly inside, closing and bolting the windows behind her as if she were keeping the devil out.

'Have you been all right alone, Bryony, dear?'

'I haven't been exactly alone. Rafe came round.'

'Rafe? But you told him you didn't want to see him.'

'That's why he came round. He decided to invite himself to dinner.'

Etta looked alarmed. 'Did you let him stay?'

'No.' Bryony shook her head. 'But I've been thinking about why he came, why he asked me out in the first place.'

'But surely he admired you and wanted to. . .' Etta frowned as she looked at Bryony. 'What reason do you think?'

'I think he wanted to get me to spy on you for him.'

'Oh, dear.' Etta sat down on a pretty gilt chair. 'Do you really think he'd do something like that?'

'I'm sure of it. He already has people spying on you;

he told me himself that he knew that you were going to the cocktail party and that you would be going on to dinner with friends. How could he possibly have known that?'

'Quite easily, really. You see, the party was in aid of a charity, and one of the organisers mentioned that Rafe had been invited, but he didn't go, of course, just sent a donation instead. And a lot of my friends were there, so it wouldn't have been difficult for him to find out if I'd been invited to dinner afterwards. There's quite a small social circle in this area, you know.'

'OK, but if Rafe went to the trouble of finding that out then he's obviously interested in your activities. He knew you'd gone to London, for example.'

'Yes, that's true. But to try to get *you* to spy on me. . .' Etta looked quite stricken. 'What did he say to you?'

'He keeps trying to find out what connection I have with you, how long I'm staying here, that kind of thing. He knows we're loosely connected by marriage, but that's all. I haven't told him why I'm here, or anything like that.'

'He's bound to be curious, I suppose. And he might start getting suspicious if we're not careful.' Getting up, Etta went over to the tray and poured herself a Cointreau. 'It might be an idea if we could fob him off with some story that would satisfy him,' she said musingly.

'We could say that I came over here to improve my Italian,' Bryony suggested.

'Yes, but if that was the only reason, then won't he think it strange that you didn't come right out and say so in the first place?' Tentatively Etta added, 'Of course we could always tell him the truth.'

'About the hotel? But I thought you didn't want him to know.'

'Of course I don't. No, I meant we could tell him the

truth about you. That you've just broken off with Jeff and have come here to try and get over him.' She gave Bryony a straight look. 'That *is* one of the main reasons why you're here, isn't it?'

'Very likely,' Bryony admitted stiffly. 'But it isn't something that I particularly want the whole of Sicily knowing — and especially Rafe.'

'But it would solve our problem by completely diverting his suspicion and curiosity, wouldn't it?' Etta said persuasively.

'Etta!' Bryony looked at her in frustrated annoyance. 'I don't want everyone to think I'm a lovesick wimp, because I'm not.'

'No, of course not. But no one in Sicily knows you, so what does it matter what they think?'

Rafe knows me. The thought came unbidden into Bryony's mind. But what did she care what he thought? He was just an arrogant, interfering nuisance they could well do without. And, as Etta said, this was a perfect way to get him off their backs. Reluctantly she nodded. 'I suppose it is the best way.'

Etta came over and hugged her. 'My dear, that's marvellous. I'm sure it will work.'

'But you can't come right out and tell him.'

'Of course not. There are much easier ways than that. I'm having a committee meeting for another charity here in a couple of days. All women, of course. We'll let them catch sight of you and they're bound to ask me who you are. I can tell them then — in strictest confidence, you understand.' She chuckled gleefully. 'It will be all round Catania within a couple of days.'

Bryony couldn't help smiling. 'Have you no respect for our sex, Etta?'

'Generally I have very little respect for either sex, my dear, just for a few individuals whom I know and love.' She yawned behind her hand. 'I'm tired. I think

I'll go up.' She kissed Bryony on the cheek. 'Thank you
so much, my dear girl. I'm sorry if this goes against the
grain, but hopefully it will satisfy Rafe's curiosity so
that he leaves us alone. See you tomorrow. Sleep well.'

But Bryony didn't sleep well. Talking about Jeff had
brought him back to her mind again. She often thought
about him, wondering what he was doing, whether he'd
gone back to the flat yet and found all her things gone,
and what his reaction had been. It was only natural that
she hoped he'd feel upset and wish they'd never split
up, realise that he'd made the biggest mistake of his
life. Then, masochistically, she thought that he'd probably met someone else by now and had completely
forgotten her.

She turned restlessly, feeling lonely and miserable.
But she was an optimist by nature and tried to concentrate on the future, not on the past. And it now seemed
that there had definitely been no future with Jeff.
Perhaps he'd done her a favour by bringing everything
to a head. After all, if she'd still been in love with Jeff
she would never have felt that surge of attraction for
Rafe.

That thought brought her fully awake, her skin
prickling. How stupidly susceptible she must be to have
let his kiss get to her. Or was it the kiss? Wasn't it
Rafe's sheer masculinity, the thought of how beautiful
his body must be beneath the civilised veneer of clothes,
his strength, and his lean good looks? Just a primitive
attraction, that was all it was. Woman's basic need for
a strong and beautiful mate. Caveman images came
into her mind of Rafe in a loincloth. He'd look pretty
good, she had to admit, but somehow she couldn't
imagine him settling into domestic bliss with any
woman. He'd walk out as soon as the woman started
looking for a permanent cave. Just the way Jeff had

done. But then—they were both men, weren't they? she thought with bitter irony.

Etta's friends came for afternoon tea, English-style, two days later. They were all Sicilian ladies and enjoyed the foreignness of the occasion. Bryony didn't join them but they saw her from the windows as she walked in the garden. It all worked perfectly, just as they'd planned, Etta reported after the women had gone. 'They were only mildly curious, but I became very mysterious, refusing to tell them anything about you, until they were begging to know. Then I swore them to secrecy, to make sure it will be all over town by tomorrow.'

'So that's the last we'll see of Rafe.'

'I certainly hope so,' Etta said fervently.

Bryony smiled in agreement, but felt a strange surge of disappointment, quickly shrugged off.

Their first guests were due to arrive that weekend, and she busied herself with taking an inventory of all the linen in the house, the cutlery and china, and the food in the larder. In the evenings she made dinner, making sure she was adapting the local produce to her recipes correctly, and everything seemed to be going perfectly—until Etta dropped her bombshell. They were in the sitting-room after dinner one evening, Bryony writing menus, Etta reading letters, when the latter suddenly let out a shrill shriek.

Bryony jumped a mile and turned to stare at her in alarm. 'What is it?'

'This letter is from our first guests, confirming their arrival times, and he says—he says. . .' Etta gave Bryony a stricken look. 'He says he wants the services of a guide to show them the island.'

'So what's wrong with that?' Bryony said in bewilderment.

'Most of the guides are on retainers to tour companies or hotels. It will be almost impossible to get one at such short notice. And if they talked to our guests the guide would soon find out that we're running the place as a hotel, then it would be all over the island, and——'

'And Rafe would find out,' Bryony finished for her, her voice hollow.

'Yes! What on earth are we going to do?'

'Could you ask them not to tell the guide, say instead that they're your guests of something?'

'I can hardly do that.' Putting down the letter, Etta poured herself a drink. 'I have to think.'

'Isn't there a guide you could trust to keep your secret?'

'I don't know any.' Sitting in an armchair, Etta brooded for several minutes, but then her brow cleared. 'Of course, the answer's simple.'

'It is?'

'Yes.' Etta gave her a beaming smile. 'You speak Italian, so *you* can be their guide.'

'You're crazy!' Bryony exclaimed, jumping to her feet. 'I don't even know the island.'

'Well, nor do they. You can read up about it and then take them.'

'I've got a better idea. Why don't you take them?'

'I don't speak Italian. Guides are always young and pretty. And, besides, it would look very odd of a hotel proprietor to act as a guide. Whereas you would be just perfect.'

'Etta, listen to me,' Bryony said firmly, cutting through her enthusiasm. 'It's impossible. A guide has to be familiar with where they're going. And I'm supposed to be the chef here; how can I possibly do two jobs?'

'You could just take them in the mornings and make sure you're back in plenty of time to do the cooking for dinner. And they wouldn't want to go every day. He says in his letter they intend to hire a vehicle big enough to take them all and they will want a guide as required.'

Bryony's mind whirled, but then she snapped her fingers. 'I've got it! Giovanni. He speaks English. He can be their guide and act as chauffeur at the same time.'

Etta gave her an eloquent look. 'Giovanni is an excellent houseman, but can you really imagine him as a guide from a select hotel? And, besides, I need him here.'

It was true, Bryony had to admit; Giovanni was good at what he did, he had been in service all his working life and was used to taking orders, but it was impossible to imagine him taking charge of a group of visiting Americans and showing them the sights of Sicily. 'But I don't know anything about Sicily, and I haven't been anywhere myself yet,' Bryony protested, knowing that she was already beaten.

'Well, that's easily remedied. You have three days, four probably because I doubt if they'll want to go anywhere on their first day here. You can read up on the places they'll want to visit and then go and see them for yourself.'

'You make it all sound so simple,' Bryony said dolefully, rapidly coming to realise that Etta could twist her round her finger.

'It is, dear. All you have to do is keep one jump ahead of them.' She got briskly to her feet. 'Now, there should be several books here on the history of Sicily, although they're probably in Italian. You can mug up on the general history and then tomorrow you can go to Mount Etna; all the visitors always want to go there first. And just think,' she added encouragingly, 'what a marvellous opportunity this will be for you to see the island.'

So Bryony found herself later that night sitting up in

bed with a stack of books on the bedside table. Most of them went deeply into the history of the island, but what she needed was a potted version that she could remember easily. She found it in a little modern travel guide, but even then it wasn't simple as Sicily had a long and violent history. Right back to the Neolithic period people had come from other places to settle on the island, and it had been occupied in turn by the Greeks, Romans, Arabs, Normans, and Spanish before it had at last been freed by Garibaldi and had become part of Italy.

Her head reeling with names and dates, Bryony turned the light out as the clock in her room chimed one and fell instantly asleep, but the next morning was up early to go to Mount Etna. Giovanni drove her in the unmistakable Rolls-Royce that had belonged to Etta's husband, the estate car having gone into the garage for repair. He opened the back door for her but she insisted on sitting beside him in the front, as she would if she were really a guide. Giovanni had a map of the island and she held it on her lap, memorising the route as they went through the nearby village, people on their way to school or work stopping to watch as the car swept by. Skirting the nearby town of Catania, Giovanni headed for the mountain that rose in the distance, the largest active volcano in Europe, its peak capped with snow, and from its summit the drifting cloud of smoke that was the constant warning of the molten fires deep within the rock.

The day was clear, and the views as they climbed the foothills breathtaking in their beauty. They passed through lush groves of citrus fruit trees — oranges, tangerines and lemons — and higher up Bryony recognised oak trees and umbrella pines as the orchards gave way to forest. The snows were melting, filling the hundreds of little waterfalls to overflowing, revealing the now

barren terrain of hardened lava with only the occasional
wild flower that thrust its head up through the black
cinders. When they reached the end of the road
Giovanni parked the car near the complex of tourist
restaurants and Bryony put on the boots and thick coat
that she'd brought with her, but even so she found the
air immediately struck chill as she got out of the car.

There were few visitors taking the cable-cars today,
just some people with skis, dressed in fashionable
Italian ski suits that made Bryony green with envy. She
went on alone, Giovanni adamantly refusing to go with
her as he didn't like heights, and sat in the glass-
windowed car, her back to the mountain, fascinated by
the panoramic view that gradually widened as they rose
higher. The car clanged into the top station and she got
out to find herself surrounded by snow. But she was
much nearer to the summit here and could smell the
sulphur and see the smoke rising from the crater. Fire
and ice. Elements so far apart but in such dangerous
proximity here on the volcano.

Etta had told her that there were special tank-tracked
buses that took visitors from here to the summit, but
when Bryony enquired she was told that they didn't
operate so early in the year. This was as far as she could
go for the present.

Taking advantage of the lack of visitors, she chatted
to the man who worked the cable-cars, who told her
about the anoraks and boots people could hire so that
they could walk up towards the very edge of the crater
if they wished. His assistant came along and obligingly
showed her a large building backing on to the mountain, previously used as an Alpine Club hostel for
climbers, that had been destroyed in the last eruption
only a few years ago. With its covering of snow, from a
distance it appeared intact, but when she looked
through the windows Bryony could see that the rooms

were filled with now solid lava, only the walls having resisted its pervasive flow. A strong smell of sulphur still pervaded the air despite the cold. She shivered, finding it spooky, and remembered a description of the mountain in one of the books she'd read last night: 'a Garden of Eden interrupted in places by a stretch of Hell'. What must it be like, she wondered, to live under this constant menace of dreadful, primitive annihilation? Turning away, she was glad to descend again, find Giovanni in a café, and join him in a cup of piping hot coffee.

After thoroughly exploring the facilities available at the lower cable-car station, Bryony bought a book and a video on Mount Etna, to satisfy her own fascination as much as to help her as a guide.

'Where to now, *signorina*?' Giovanni asked as he waited patiently by the car.

Bryony consulted her travel guide and caught sight of the name Taormina. That was the place that Rafe had offered to take her to see. She hesitated, then said, 'Some lunch, I think, and then to Taormina, please.'

Over their meal Bryony practised her Italian by asking Giovanni questions about the island, but found that he knew very little and preferred to talk about Rome, where he and Maria had been brought up.

'Don't you like living here?' she asked him.

'Oh, yes, it is very pleasant, but it is so quiet, you understand, after Rome.'

The area of the villa was quiet, Bryony had to admit, but she found the towns, with their racing streams of traffic, very noisy. But when she said as much to Giovanni, he shook his head emphatically. 'No, no! Compared to Rome these towns are villages.'

The ride along the *autostrada* past the coastal resorts with their concrete wall of hotels was pleasant enough, but the journey became really interesting as they took

the twisting road that climbed to Taormina. Bryony
hadn't expected the town to be so high, but she
discovered that it was over six hundred feet up.

The afternoon was really warm, especially after the
chill of Mount Etna. Getting out of the car, Bryony
took off her jacket. 'I'm afraid I don't know how long
I'll be,' she told him.

'Is no problem. Please, take as long as you want.'

Bryony had intended to go straight to the famous
Greek theatre that was the little town's best known
tourist attraction, but she took one look at the pretty
streets, lined with boutiques and shops full of ceramics
and jewellery, and she was lured into them, forgetting
all about the theatre. Even now, in the early spring,
there were plenty of people walking along, sitting at the
café tables in tree-filled piazzas, or pausing to admire
the view between the buildings of the long sweep of
coastline below.

It was her parents' wedding anniversary in a couple
of weeks, so Bryony took great pleasure in going round
the shops, looking for something they would like. There
were so many beautiful things that she was spoilt for
choice, but eventually chose a set of silver napkin rings
that would be easy to post. She also bought a bottle of
the local almond wine which she sampled in a shop and
thought she might be able to use in some of her
recipes — and a pair of the most gorgeous Italian shoes
that were more than she could afford but found impossible to resist.

Coming out of the shoe shop, she found that the day
had started to cool and she put on her jacket, then
remembered that she was supposed to be visiting the
theatre. Quickly she hurried back through the town and
up the wide street leading to the site. Thankfully the
gate was still open. Bryony paid her money and went
in, following the path that rose in a flight of steps, then

caught her breath as she came out into an open area
and saw the best view yet of the coastline. Going to a
rail that guarded the path, she stood looking out at the
bay spread out before her, drinking it in, wishing she
had a camera.

Footsteps crunched on the path and climbed the
stairs behind her. She went to move on, then became
still as she glanced down and saw that it was Rafe. He
had known it was her; there was no surprise on his face
as he came up to join her. 'There's a much better view
further up,' he remarked, and fell into step beside her
as if they had been together the whole afternoon.

Not at all sure how she felt, Bryony didn't say
anything, just let him lead her up into the ruins of the
theatre. He paused in the entrance so that she could
take in the tiers of seats and what was left of the classic
columns that had graced the stage. Then he put a hand
under her elbow to help her to climb the uneven flight
of stairs between the seats towards the top.

'I can manage,' Bryony said shortly, pulling her arm
away.

She was almost at the top before she paused and
looked round, then gave a gasp of wonder. 'Oh!' she
murmured on a long sigh. The brick ruins, rosy in the
dying sunlight, were immediately below her, then there
was a stretch of deep green cypresses, and beyond and
far below them the curving outline of the blue waters
of the bay stretching away into the mists of the horizon.

Rafe touched her arm and nodded to the right. 'Look
over there.'

She turned her head and saw Mount Etna, its white-
capped summit seeming to float in the sky, its base lost
in the evening mists. Slowly she sank down on to one
of the stone seats, aware that others had sat there and
seen this view for over two thousand years. It was so
lovely that it caught at her heart and she felt a tear

trickle on to her cheek. Quickly she put up a hand and wiped it away, not wanting Rafe to see.

But luckily he began to talk about the theatre, telling her when it was built and something of its history. 'It's still used,' he added. 'They put on classical plays, and even films during the film festival.'

That made her laugh. 'How prosaic.'

'Yes.' He turned to look at her. 'Are you all right now?'

So he had noticed. Damn! 'How did you know I was here?' she asked stiffly.

'Everyone comes to Taormina, and everyone who comes to Taormina comes to the theatre,' he said lightly.

'That doesn't answer my question.'

'No.' He shrugged. 'Someone noticed you going out in the car.'

'Your spy in the village,' she stated coldly.

'Yes,' Rafe admitted, taking her by surprise, making her quickly turn to look at him. 'I like to know what Etta is up to.'

Putting that aside for the moment, she said, 'And I suppose you guessed I'd come here.'

But he shook his head. 'I expected you to, and I had somone on the lookout for the car. He telephoned me when you arrived.'

She gazed at him, wondering why he should have gone to such lengths to find out where she went, and then had followed her. Well, there was only one way to find out. 'Why?' she demanded bluntly.

His mouth quirked. 'An Italian woman wouldn't have asked that question. She would have taken it for granted that I wanted to see her again, to be with her — because I was attracted to her,' he added steadily.

'But I'm not Italian. And I know that isn't the reason.'

'Do you?' Rafe gave her an enigmatic look.

'Yes.' Bryony stood up. 'I'm quite sure that the only reason you want to be — with me, as you put it, is because you want me to spy on Etta for you.' She put her hands on her hips and glowered down at him, her voice rising in anger. 'Well, I can tell you here and now that I have no intention of doing your dirty work for you! I like Etta. I like her a lot. And I think that the way you're trying to drive her out of her home by spying on her and stealing her money is despicable. *Ignobile*,' she said in Italian so that he wouldn't miss the point. 'So you can stop following me around. I'm not going to do anything for you and I never want to see you again. Do you hear me?'

'Perfectly,' Rafe answered calmly. 'I forgot to tell you how good the acoustics are here; I think everyone in Taormina heard you.'

Bryony blinked and glanced quickly round, seeing that the few people left in the theatre were all looking at her. Her face flushing with embarrassment, she ran towards the steps, but Rafe came after her and caught her arm.

'You'll break your ankle if you run on these stones,' he warned her.

She rounded on him furiously. 'Will you please leave me alone?'

He looked down at her for a long moment, still grasping her arm, then he shook his head. 'No, I don't think I will.' Tucking her arm through his and holding it firmly, he began to walk back down the steps, making her go with him. 'I think that I'm going to do as I intended.'

'Which is?' she demanded hotly.

'To take you out to dinner.'

'I've already told you I don't want to — '

'But I really must insist,' Rafe interrupted. 'I know a

very good restaurant here where they serve the most delicious seafood. Now, you wouldn't want to miss that, would you?'

'If it meant eating with you, then yes, any time,' Bryony retorted.

They had reached the gate at the entrance to the theatre and he began to walk down the street towards the square where Giovanni was waiting with the Rolls. His hold relaxed a little and she quickly pulled her arm away.

'Don't you ever listen, Signor Cavalleri? I don't want to have dinner with you.'

'You must call me Raphael,' he told her. 'Or even Rafe, as Etta does.'

'There are a whole lot of names I could call you,' she said tartly, 'but Rafe isn't one of them. Goodbye.' And she swung on her heel to hurry ahead of him to the place where Giovanni had parked.

Dusk was gathering now and the street-lamps had come on. A line of cars was parked in the square, but the wide bulk of the Rolls wasn't among them. Bryony came to a stop and stared round her in consternation. Darn, she must have come to the wrong square! But then she recognised the café on the corner and the shop selling traditional puppets that she had gone into earlier. A terrible suspicion entered her mind and she turned to look at Rafe who had calmly followed her. He nodded. 'Yes, I sent him home — so now you have no choice but to join me for dinner, do you?'

CHAPTER FOUR

'I DON'T believe you.' Bryony looked wildly round. 'Giovanni wouldn't just abandon me.'

'No, but I told him that Etta wanted him back at the villa and she had asked me to bring you home,' Rafe told her quite calmly.

Her eyes full of scorn, she said, 'You lied to him.'

Rafe gave her a rueful smile and said, 'How else could I get you to have dinner with me?' his tone making it sound almost as if it were her fault.

Taking a deep breath, Bryony strove to control her temper. 'You might be able to get away with this sort of high-handed behaviour with other women, but——'

'But there is no other woman that I want to have dinner with,' he interruptd outrageously.

Completely unmoved, Bryony said, 'Do you really think that kind of—of fulsome flattery is going to get you anywhere?'

'Obviously not.' Rafe sighed. 'How fiery you are.' Then, in a more serious tone, he said, 'Bryony, you have heard a great many things about me from Etta, all of them to my discredit, I know. Don't you think that I should be allowed to tell you my side of the story?'

'No, I don't.'

His eyebrows rose. 'You are not willing to be fair?'

'I don't know why you should *want* to tell *me* your version,' she corrected him. 'What do you care what I think of you?'

His eyes settled on her face and for a moment she thought that he was going to tell her that he did care, or make some other smooth-tongued remark to flatter and cajole her. Her chin came up, her eyes filling with scorn, which quickly deflated when he shrugged and said, 'I don't, of course. But Etta's dislike of me makes her exaggerate. She has the fixed idea that I'm her enemy and won't listen to me when I try to talk to her and explain things. And she has friends in Sicily to whom she doesn't hesitate to vilify me, which sometimes makes it uncomfortable for me and the rest of my family.' He gave her a deprecatory smile. 'I hoped that, if I explained the position to you, you might in turn be able to persuade Etta to listen to me. So I appeal to your British sense of justice to hear my side of the story,' he finished lightly.

He was so smooth, sounded so reasonable, that Bryony hesitated. It was true that she'd only heard Etta's version. And, let's face it, she thought, I've only known Etta for a few weeks. Maybe she does exaggerate, perhaps even gets things out of proportion in her own mind. When her husband died she might have been too upset to understand how things really were left. But she still hesitated. 'Whatever is between you and Etta,' she said at length, 'is really none of my business.'

'But haven't you made it your business, by showing how much you dislike me?' Rafe protested. 'It's perfectly obvious that you've let Etta influence you against me.'

Which was true, although Bryony also thought him much too arrogant for anyone to like him. To be attracted to him, yes, but to *like* him?

'Why don't you talk to her through your solicitors?' she countered.

He shrugged expressively, lifting his hands in a hopeless show of despair, a gesture so Italian that she almost smiled. 'Etta's lawyers scent a lucrative battle; when I try to go through them I get nowhere. It would

be much better to talk to her face to face, but only if
she's willing to listen.'

'Which is where I come in,' Bryony said drily.

'If you are Etta's friend, yes.'

She made a derisive sound. 'If I'm willing to act as
your go-between, you mean.'

He gave a genuine smile then. 'Do you always insist
on speaking so plainly, Bryony?'

'Is there any point in doing otherwise?'

'Perhaps not. Will you help me?'

'So that the local ladies won't have such a poor
opinion of you?' she said on a slightly disdainful note.

'So that they won't have an untrue one,' he corrected
her. Adding, 'Or you.'

'You've said that my opinion doesn't matter to you,'
she pointed out lightly.

His lips quirked a little. 'Will you listen to me over
dinner?'

'I'll telephone Etta.'

'To tell her you'll be late home?'

'To ask her how she feels about me listening to you.
I'm her guest,' she pointed out. 'I won't go behind her
back.'

Rafe nodded, an amused glint in his eyes. 'What
more could I hope for?' he said lightly. Then he
gestured towards the main street. 'We'll find a telephone this way.'

The town wasn't so crowded now, although the shops
were still open, their well-lit windows enticing. They
didn't talk as they walked along, but Bryony noticed
the many glances they drew from the passers-by, both
men and women. She wasn't so used to attracting notice
herself; in London she was just one good-looking girl
among thousands, and nor was she used to having the
man she was with draw so many eyes. Jeff had been
quite handsome, in a very English kind of way, with

brown hair and open features; but Rafe had the kind of looks men envied and women dreamed about. And he was tall, too, much taller than most Sicilian men seemed to be.

Turning to him, she said, 'Why are you so tall?'

Rafe laughed at the bluntness of the question. 'Do you know anything about Sicilian history?'

'A little.'

'Then you will probably have read how the island was conquered by the Normans in the eleventh century. My family is descended from that time. Our name is thought to be a corruption of the word *chevalier* or cavalier. I have some Spanish blood in my veins, too. But then most Sicilians are probably a mixture of races.'

They had come to a sloping side-street off to the left and he led her down it, past an open space and into the entrance of a hotel. The doorman greeted him by name as he held the door wide.

'You will find a telephone over there.' Rafe pointed. 'I'll wait for you in the bar; the receptionist will show you the way when you've finished the call.'

'What makes you think I won't just call a taxi?' she asked curiously.

Picking up her hand, he bowed slightly over it. 'I'll just have to trust you — as I hope you will trust me.'

Etta answered the phone almost at once, and when she heard Bryony's voice said, 'My dear, where are you? I was *furious* with Giovanni for believing Rafe. Shall I send the car to rescue you?'

'I'm not sure. Rafe says that he wants to talk to me about — well, about the differences between the two of you. He seems to want me to act as some kind of mediator between you. He says that you don't understand his position and ——'

'Oh, don't I?' Etta snorted.

Bryony laughed. 'I had an idea that's how you'd feel.

Shall I get a taxi home or shall I listen to him? I don't want to interfere, Etta, or hear things you'd rather I didn't, but apart from that what have you got to lose?'

'That's true. And I suppose it might be amusing to hear what lies he tells you.' Bryony was silent, making Etta say quickly, 'You haven't let him get to you, have you? I know he can be very persuasive, slanting the truth to his own ends.'

'Of course not. I'm quite willing to come home if you want me to. It's entirely up to you.'

'Stay, then,' Etta said decisively. 'You might even learn something useful. Although I doubt it; Rafe is far too clever to give anything away. Where are you?'

'I don't know exactly. Some hotel in Taormina. "The San Domenico Palace",' she read from a notice in the booth.

Etta laughed. 'That's *some* hotel; it's one of the best on the island. I won't send the car for you; Rafe will bring you home. Goodbye, Bryony—and don't let him influence you against me.'

Somewhat surprised that Etta was willing for her to stay, and even more that she wasn't going to send the car for her, Bryony put down the receiver with a frown, wondering why. There was a small mirror in the booth; catching sight of her reflection in it, Bryony decided that the next thing was to find the ladies' room. Among Bryony's contemporaries there was a widely held belief that you could always tell how classy a place was by the ladies' room, and this hotel certainly lived up to its five-star rating. Having been out since early morning, she took her time, washing her face and hands in a marble basin, redoing her make-up and brushing her hair before the gilt mirrors, and adding some scent from the bottle of Givenchy in her bag. If Rafe was willing to go to these lengths to talk to her then he could darn well wait, she thought, standing in front of the mirror and swirling her hair about her head. She wished she weren't wearing trousers, but at least they were quite smart black ones rather than her usual jeans; hardly the right clothes for a place like this, though.

The receptionist pointed out the way to the bar and she went out of the foyer into a huge square area, its centre a garden full of trees and plants, its stone-columned edges glassed in but forming a walk all round. Bryony stood looking round in surprise for a few minutes before she went through another door into the huge, lofty room that formed the bar. Rafe was sitting on a comfortable settee, a small table with a glass on it in front of him. He rose as she came up to him, apparently in no way put out by his long wait.

But Bryony couldn't resist saying, 'Did you think I wasn't coming?'

But he ducked that one, merely smiling and saying, 'I'm glad you're here. I take it Etta gave her permission. She's probably curious to know what I have to say.' He indicated the place beside him and Bryony sat down, but not too close. 'What would you like to drink?'

'Gin and tonic, please.'

'A very English drink.' Lifting a finger to the watching waiter, he gave the order.

'This is an amazing place,' Bryony observed.

'Yes, it used to be a convent. This room was the refectory and the garden area you came through was the sixteenth-century cloister. There used to be a church as well, but unfortunately the place was used as a German headquarters in the war and the Allies bombed it.'

'That's a shame,' Bryony murmured, and smiled at the waiter who put her drink on the table in front of her.

'Yes.' Something in Rafe's tone made her glance at

him, but he bent forward to pick up his own drink and said, 'What did you think of Mount Etna?'

'How did you know I——?' She broke off and her chin came up. 'I suppose someone there happened to see the car and tell you,' she said caustically.

'No. I asked Giovanni and he said he'd taken you there this morning.'

'Oh.' Bryony thought of apologising but didn't. Answering his question, she said, 'I found the mountain—awesome. It made me realise how small and puny man is when compared to such a violent force of nature. That there's nothing that can be done to hold it back if the volcano erupts.'

'They call it the forge of Vulcan,' Rafe remarked. 'But you haven't seen it at its most impressive. You should go there when most of the snow has melted, ideally before dawn when you can go to the crater's edge and see the lava glowing red with heat. And smell the sulphur, and see the colours in the crater walls caused by the transmuted gases. And then turn away from the dark, primitive forces, and see the whole of Sicily spread before you as the sun rises. That is an unforgettable experience.'

'Yes, I suppose it would be,' Bryony agreed, her eyes fixed on his face, surprised that he should show so much sensitivity, be so aware of natural beauty.

'If you stay long enough in Sicily, I'll take you up to see it,' Rafe remarked, then raised his eyebrow enquiringly at her. 'Do you think you will still be in Sicily in the summer?'

Searching for an answer, Bryony remembered that by now he would probably have heard that she was here to get over a broken romance. Maybe he'd thought that was why she'd cried in the theatre. Looking down at her drink, she said, 'I don't know. I—— My plans are uncertain.'

He nodded, accepting the ambiguousness, convincing her that he had heard about Jeff.

Thinking that finding out information could work two ways, she said, 'Do you live in Sicily all the time?'

'No, I also spend a lot of time in Rome. Have you been there?'

'No, I haven't.'

'It's well worth the journey. Perhaps you could go on there for a few days before you go back to England. There are plenty of flights from here every day.'

'I'll bear it in mind,' she said lightly.

'Persuade Etta to take you; she likes Rome.'

'How long for—a couple of months?' Bryony asked baldly, becoming tired of this polite fencing. 'Then you could get your house back from Etta. That's what you want, isn't it?'

Rafe shook his head sadly. 'Such directness. In Italy we take our time over these things.'

'Do you? But in our case we have nothing in common, so why waste time?'

He gestured eloquently. 'Who knows? We may find that we have many things in common.'

Bryony laughed. 'I doubt that very much.'

His gaze was fixed on her face, an arrested expression in his eyes, for so long that Bryony said wryly, 'Have I got another speck on my face or something?'

He blinked and grinned, a real grin of genuine amusement. '*Mi scusi*. I was just thinking how some women don't look beautiful until their face is in repose, and others until they laugh.' He didn't have to add the obvious compliment, his eloquent silence had said it all.

Wow! Bryony picked up her drink and took a long swallow to hide her confused thoughts. This is getting heavy, she thought wryly. Does he really believe I go for all that?

As if he guessed her thoughts, Rafe grinned again.

'Why is it that Englishwomen are always suspicious of compliments? Can it be because Englishmen are so seldom in the habit of making them, I wonder?'

'At least when they make them they mean them,' Bryony said in quick defence of her countrymen.

'What makes you think I don't?' He said it in a serious tone that she didn't know how to answer, but she didn't have to because he stood up. 'Shall we go to dinner?'

He left some money on the table for the drinks and held open the door to the covered cloister for her. Bryony had expeced them to eat there and gave him a look of surprise when he led her out of the hotel.

'We'll dine there some other time,' he explained 'We're not dressed for it tonight.'

She certainly wasn't, but Rafe, in his dark, well-cut suit, looked good enough to dine anywhere. So he was being tactful, and that she appreciated. They walked back down the main street, fuller now with people out for an evening stroll, to a restaurant that was built like a terrace overlooking the sea, and had the most marvellous view out across the bay. The waiter led them to a table right by the huge windows, almost as if that particular table had been reserved for them, and Bryony turned to look out at the thousands of lights that drew the outline of the coast.

It caught her breath, made her remember another view in another place, when she had been with Jeff. Inner anger made her turn quickly away and say to Rafe acidly, 'Do you always keep this table reserved in case you pick up a stray woman?'

He had been looking at her expectantly, but now Rafe's face hardened. 'Of course — if that is how you think of yourself.'

Ouch! She'd thrown herself on the point of that one. Bryony lifted her hand to push her hair out of the way, and sighed. 'I'm sorry. I — I was thinking of something else.'

'And someone else, perhaps?'

She gave him a quick glance, then looked away. 'Perhaps.'

The waiter came up with the menus and spoke to her in Italian, recommending a swordfish steak. Bryony automatically replied in the same language, settling for the swordfish for the main course and *pasta con sarde*, a speciality of the island that she was eager to learn how to make, as a starter.

Rafe gave his order and said, 'Milan? Yes?'

'I'm sorry?'

'You learnt to speak Italian in Milan, I think. Your accent is very fluent but correct. Like —— ' he groped for the right words ' — Oxford English. Do I have that correctly?'

'Word perfect,' she assured him, with only a trace of irony. His English was much too good to mock; much better than her Italian. 'I originally learnt at college, but yes, I went to Milan for six months to study the language.' She looked rueful. 'I wasn't aware that I spoke so un-idiomatically.'

'Only an Italian would notice,' he assured her. 'Why did you learn?'

'I had some idea of using languages in a career, but . . .well, it didn't happen that way.'

'What did you do instead?'

'Nothing very much.' Avoiding his swift glance, she said, 'Is that the wine menu? Do you think we could have a local wine? Etta doesn't seem to have much in her cellars.'

'No, my uncle preferred to lay down French and German wines. He always bought the Sicilian wines as he needed them from local merchants.'

There he went again, stressing that the house had

been his uncle's, refusing to acknowledge Etta's ownership. 'Why do you dislike Etta so much?' she asked
straight out.

Picking up his champagne aperitif, Rafe looked down
at the delicate crystal flute, twisting it in his long fingers,
his face contemplative. Bryony thought that he wasn't
going to answer, that he had found the blunt question
too rude and personal. But then he surprised her by
saying, 'I don't dislike Etta. As a matter of fact I rather
admire her. I think that's she's a very clever woman.'

'Do Italian men really admire brainy women?'

He smiled at that. 'I didn't say intellectual—just
clever.' An ambiguous statement that he evidently
didn't intend to explain.

'You said that you wanted to tell me your version,'
she pointed out when he didn't go on.

He nodded, but seemed to be in no hurry, sitting
back in his chair and sipping his drink. 'Will you visit
Milan while you're in Italy?'

'I shouldn't think so.'

'Have you no friends there?'

'Some. But I haven't been back for over two years.'

'Really? What have you been doing in that time?'

She suddenly saw where his questions were leading;
he was trying to find out about her broken affair. 'I've
been in England,' she said unhelpfully.

'And not using your languages.'

'That's right.'

Annoyed by his curiosity, Bryony was determined
not to give anything away, and short of coming right
out and asking her there was little more he could find
out. He must have realised it himself, because Rafe
suddenly put down his glass and said crisply, 'My
parents were killed in a car crash when I was very small
and I was brought up by my uncle. I looked upon him
as a father. The villa was my home.' He shrugged. 'I

was sent away to school, of course, and then I went to university in Rome and business school in America. But I always looked on the villa as my home and went back there often. Uncle Antonio's wife died in childbirth before I was born, and he never showed any signs of wishing to marry again. But then he came to visit me in Rome — and I introduced him to Etta.'

'You did?' Bryony exclaimed in surprise.

'Yes. She was — an acquaintance. My uncle had been unwell. Etta persuaded him to go on a long cruise. I thought it was a good idea, until I found that she had gone along, too.'

'Why was that so bad?'

Rafe flicked her a glance but went on, 'When they came back she went to live with him, and then —— ' He paused, seemed to deliberate over what he was going to say, but merely finished, 'Then he decided to marry her.' He smiled thinly. 'He was a very stubborn old man; nothing I could say would dissuade him.'

'Why should you want to?'

He gave her a contemplative look, then shook his head. 'You wouldn't understand.'

'Try me,' she invited.

'It was a matter of — family pride.'

For a moment she couldn't think what he meant, then her face hardened. 'You mean you didn't think Etta was good enough to marry into your family, is that it?'

He didn't deny it, but said, 'With Etta as the owner the villa is closed to me. I am unable to use it as my ancestors have done for more than the last two centuries: as our home, the place where we can entertain friends and neighbours, the centre of our family, owned and run by its head. For the first time in nearly three hundred years the Casa dei Cavalleri is no longer the family home.' His voice hardened. 'Instead it is in the hands of a——' He broke off abruptly, his eyes going to her as if remembering who he was with. 'In the hands of a foreigner.'

He had spoken vehemently, almost passionately, and Bryony could see that it did, indeed, mean a lot to him. All Italians, she knew, had a great sense of family, and she had an idea that this was probably even stronger among Sicilians. It must be galling for Rafe to have become the head of the family but not to have the use of the ancestral home. But she couldn't forgive him for his snobbery over Etta. So her voice was cold when she said, 'What do you want me to tell Etta?'

He straightened up, his face losing its intensity. The waiters came with the first course, with the wine, white and made from the grapes grown on Mount Etna. Rafe waited until they'd gone before he said, 'I have tried to explain to her how deeply I feel. I have made her a substantial offer to give up the house, enough to keep her in great comfort in Rome or anywhere else she wants to live. But she refuses to listen to me.'

'Does she know that you tried to persuade your uncle not to marry her?'

'I'm afraid she does.'

Rafe's voice was rueful, but Bryony was willing to bet it was for entirely the wrong reasons; if Etta hadn't known maybe she would have accepted his offer now. 'Then I'm not surprised she won't listen to you,' she said shortly. 'I wouldn't if I were in her place.'

'But it might help if you explained how I felt.'

'I doubt it. She loves the villa, too. Who wouldn't?'

'Do you like it?'

'Of course. It's beautiful. And the gardens——' she shook her head in remembered awe '—they're perfectly lovely.' She looked up and saw that Rafe was watching her. 'Or they would be if Etta had enough money to keep them in good order,' she added bitingly. 'But she said that you have sto—*denied* her the use of the income from the orange groves and things,' she amended, not knowing the facts. 'The money that should have supported the upkeep of the house.'

'My uncle left her the use of the villa. There was no specific mention of any income for the house.'

'Did he have to be specific? Wouldn't he have taken it for granted that the money would be provided?' Bryony's tone grew sarcastic. 'Maybe your uncle would even have taken it for granted that the nephew he had taken in and raised as his own would have the common decency to take care of his widow, the woman he had loved and who had made his last years happy.'

Rafe put down his knife and fork and balled his hands into tight fists, the knuckles showing white. 'Is this what Etta has told you?' he asked harshly.

'No, it's what you've just told me. You want Etta out of that house and you're willing to make her life miserable to do it.' Bryony dropped her fork on to her plate, the food largely untouched. 'You made a mistake asking me to listen to you; all you've done is confirm what Etta has already told me.'

'She has told you what she wanted you to hear. There is a lot more that she will never tell you. Such as her—position in life, shall we call it?—when she met my uncle. And the way she tried to keep his family away from him after their marriage, and especially in his last year when he was very frail.'

'If by his family you mean you, then I'm not surprised,' Bryony retorted. 'You would probably have bullied and hectored him into an early grave.' The moment she'd said it, Bryony knew that she'd gone too far. But it was too late to draw back now. Rafe's face had paled beneath his natural tan and his mouth was drawn into a thin line of inner anger.

'I see that there is no point in talking on this subject any further,' he said curtly.

Bryony picked up her bag and went to stand up. 'I'll go, then.'

'No. Sit down. Finish your meal.'

His tone was short, peremptory, making her chin come up. 'Are you *ordering* me to?'

His lips twisted into a thin smile in which there was no humour. 'On the contrary, I wouldn't dream of ever ordering you to do anything, Miss Ferrers.'

She didn't know how to take that. Stiffly she said, 'If I've offended you I'm sorry.'

His voice as cool as her own, Rafe said, 'It is I who should apologise. You are my guest. Please sit down and finish your meal; you must be hungry.'

Bryony slowly sat down on her chair, not sure whether she wanted to go or stay. She looked at him but could read nothing in his mask-like face. He began to eat, so she did the same, but felt constrained by his silence into desperately searching for something to say and lamely coming out with, 'This pasta is very good.'

'I'm glad you like it.'

'I might try it at the villa.' The moment the words were out Bryony could have bitten her tongue, but Rafe merely raised an eyebrow and she said quickly, 'I like to cook.'

'Really?' It was a mere politeness; he didn't, couldn't, suspect anything.

'Yes,' she said thankfully. 'It—it's something to do. Maria is from Rome and doesn't know any of the local dishes.'

'No, I suppose not.'

Raising her eyes, Bryony watched him as he poured more wine into their glasses. Am I being unfair to him? she wondered. It might well be that Etta had tried to keep him away from his uncle and he had resented it.

And what was that he'd said earlier—that she should ask Etta about her position before she'd met Antonio? What on earth was that supposed to mean? Glancing across the restaurant, she saw another young couple, their heads close together as they talked, the man's hand covering the girl's. So different from their own table on which a careful guard of politeness had been put between their anger. But it would take an asbestos blanket to quench it completely, Bryony thought ruefully.

Finishing the pasta, she picked up her glass, took a sip, and looked across at Rafe. His eyes met hers briefly. 'Shall we try to find a neutral subject on which to talk?'

She smiled a little. 'Is there one?'

He shrugged. 'Between us, perhaps not. It is obvious that you look on me as an enemy—just as Etta does.'

'I don't mean to be so biased. But it's difficult not to be. And you don't make it easy,' she added accusingly.

'Don't I?'

Bryony wanted to come right out and ask him what he'd meant about Etta, but was pretty certain she'd get an equally unhelpful answer, so decided to approach the subject more subtly. 'How long have you known Etta?'

'About eight years.'

'How did you meet?'

She wasn't sure but she thought he hesitated just slightly before saying, 'Through a mutual friend.'

'In Rome?'

'Yes.'

He didn't enlarge on it and she realised she wasn't going to get anywhere that way either, so she said instead, 'What do you do in Rome?'

'I have business interests there.'

'The family business you inherited from Antonio?'

'Among others.'

'Which do you regard as your home, here or Rome?'

'Sicily always,' he said with subconscious pride and possessiveness.

'It is a beautiful island,' she acknowledged. 'Even if a dangerous one.'

'Dangerous?'

'With an active volcano hanging over you all the time it has to be dangerous.'

He looked amused. 'That makes it more exciting, makes you live your life more fully.'

'So you like living dangerously.'

His eyes came up to meet hers, their depths dark and brooding, but able to light with a fire as intense as the volcano. Bryony had seen them light like that in anger; she wondered if they lit with the same fire in love. The thought confused her and made her cheeks colour a little. She looked away, uncomfortably aware that Rafe had guessed why.

'Yes,' he agreed softly. 'And living it to the full. When I see something I want I do everything in my power to get it.'

Again her eyes were drawn to his, as if they contained a magnetic power. 'And do you always succeed?' she asked, her voice a little breathless.

Rafe smiled. 'I still haven't got the villa yet.'

She welcomed the flash of humour, was strangely glad that he could joke at his own expense. She laughed. 'So you haven't.'

It eased the tension, and when their main course came they were able to talk more easily, although Bryony had the feeling that they were both watching what they said, Bryony because of the hotel, of course—but she couldn't think why Rafe should have to guard his words.

Apart from this reserve, he set out to converse

amusingly, so that she almost enjoyed the rest of the meal. Etta's name wasn't mentioned again until they left the restaurant and began to walk back to where Rafe's sports car was waiting, gleaming in the lamp-light. She held back. 'I can easily phone Etta and ask her to send the car for me. I don't want to take you out of your way.'

'It isn't out of my way. I live in Catania.' He held the door open for her. 'You don't have to be afraid, Bryony.'

'Don't I? You made a pass at me once before,' she pointed out, somehow wanting to remind him, although angry at herself for doing so.

'Ah, but that was before I knew you.'

A remark that so surprised her that Bryony could find nothing to say. She had to stoop to get into the low car. It was lucky she was wearing trousers; she would have shown a great deal of leg if she'd had on a skirt. But the car seats were deep, luxurious leather and the engine throbbed with powerful life when Rafe started it.

'How fast does it go?' she asked.

He grinned. 'As fast as the speed-limit will allow.'

'How fast is that?'

'It varies for the engine size of the car. Up to one hundred and ten kilometres an hour for this one. Do you like speed?'

'I love it! I don't have a car, though. Not now,' she added with a slight catch in her voice. She and Jeff had shared a car but that had been left behind when she walked out. Afraid he might notice, she said quickly, 'That's why I like skiing so much.'

'It's a shame you weren't here earlier in the year, then; the skiing on Etna is good in the winter, but the snow is melting too much for it to be good now. You could try it, though.'

It wasn't 'we' any more, she noticed. He had evidently given up on trying to charm her over to his side. The twisty road down from Taormina made him drive at a moderate speed, but when they got on to the *autostrada* Rafe put his foot down and they zipped along the coast road. There was little traffic now and he was a good driver, fast but in charge of the powerful beast under his hands. Once she'd got used to them overtaking cars on the wrong side, Bryony loved it and gave a sigh of pleasure and regret when they pulled up outside the heavy gates of the villa.

'I enjoyed that,' she said sincerely.

Rafe grinned. 'Not completely. You were wishing that you were driving. I could feel it.'

'I don't think I could ever drive here; the drivers are crazy, especially in the towns.'

'They do tend to be rather impulsive,' he agreed, which she supposed was quite an admission.

He helped her out of the car and insisted on walking up to the house with her. The gates were unlocked and they walked up the drive between the banks of flowers and shrubs. Strangely, Bryony found that she was in no hurry to go in and let her steps slow. When they came to the little chapel where she had first met Rafe, she said abruptly, 'What do I tell Etta?'

She couldn't see him shrug in the darkness but guessed that he did. 'Tell her what you like. I don't suppose it will make any difference to her, as it hasn't to you.'

'That isn't so.' She stopped, hesitated for a moment as she groped for words, then said, 'I was — moved by what you said. I've tried to understand and I think I do to a certain extent. But you haven't told me everything, have you?' But he didn't answer. 'So how can I really judge? You have no right to ask me to, anyway. You said you wanted me as a messenger, but you really want me on your side. Well, I'm sorry, but I can't be.' She made an impatient, almost resentful gesture. 'I really don't want to be mixed up in this, you know. It isn't my affair.'

'No, not *your* affair,' Rafe agreed, the emphasis on the pronoun so slight that she almost missed it. 'You're right, Bryony, I ought not to have involved you. I'm sorry.' He lifted her hand slightly and bowed over it. 'Thank you for having dinner with me,' he said formally. 'And for listening to me, of course. *Arrivederci*, Bryony.'

He didn't look back. Bryony turned and walked across to the house. She didn't have a key and had to ring the bell but it was Etta who came to open it for her.

'How did it go?' she asked as soon as they were in the sitting-room.

'Weird. I don't really know why he asked me.'

'Did he ask lots of questions? Was he suspicious about the hotel?'

'No, not at all. And I think he must have heard the gossip we put out about why I'm here, because he didn't ask me much about myself either. He told me quite a lot about himself, though, about why he wants the villa.'

'What did he say?'

Sitting in a chair, Bryony cast her mind back, wanting to put over Rafe's reasons as fairly as she could. 'I think you have to realise what a strong sense of family he has, and then remember that this has been the family home for about three hundred years. He wants to rule the roost from here, but can't. I suppose it's like the British royal family being kicked out of Buckingham Palace and having the place lived in by a foreigner.'

'I was his uncle's wife; I have more right to the villa than he has.'

'Not to Rafe's way of thinking, and I'm afraid nothing will change that.' She looked up at Etta. 'I know you've refused the offer he made you to move out, but couldn't you come to some kind of compromise?'

'There isn't one — short of sharing the house, and I think both of us would rather set fire to the place than do that,' Etta answered grimly.

'You hate each other, don't you?'

The older woman crossed the room to sit on the sofa. 'Yes, I think you're right.'

Bryony looked at her curiously. 'Yet Rafe said that he's known you for years and that he actually introduced you to his uncle. He would hardly have done that if he'd hated you.'

'He told you that?' Etta looked surprised. 'No, he didn't hate me then. It was when Antonio decided to marry me and he saw his inheritance slipping away from him that he changed.'

'That's right; he said he'd tried to persuade Antonio not to.'

Etta gave a somewhat resentful laugh. 'Rafe has really taken you into his confidence, hasn't he?'

'I'm sorry if you'd rather I didn't know. I told him that I didn't want to get involved.'

'Well, it seems that you are, like it or not. What else did he tell you?' But Bryony hesitated, making Etta say shortly, 'I'd rather know, Bryony.'

'He said that you tried to keep him away from his uncle.'

'Yes, I did,' Etta admitted. 'I didn't want Antonio to be constantly pestered by business matters, or to have Rafe continually trying to turn him against me. So I forbade Rafe to come to the house, which made him hate me even more, of course. Are you shocked?'

'Good heavens, no! I told Rafe that he would probably have bullied his uncle to death.'

Etta's eyes widened. 'You did! I'm very grateful —
but I bet Rafe didn't like it.'

'No, he was furious. He said there was no point in
discussing it further and became icy cold and very
formal and polite.'

Giving a theatrical shiver, Etta said, 'I can just
imagine. So that was the end of it, was it?'

Bryony hesitated. 'More or less.'

'What else was there? You had much better say,
Bryony. I assure you I can take it.'

'Well — Rafe said that I should ask you what your —
he called it your "position" was when you met his
uncle.'

'Did he, now?' Etta got up and went over to the
mirror. Apart from being a little overweight, Etta was
still attractive; her brown hair was dark and shining,
her face unlined. 'Rafe didn't tell you himself, then?'

'No. He said to ask you.'

'Putting the onus on me. Typical.' She turned and
faced Bryony, a grim look on her face. 'I was the friend
of a business associate of Rafe's — a *particularly* close
friend,' she emphasised.

'You were his mistress.' Bryony made it a flat statement, without inflexion.

'Yes. And when Rafe found out that his uncle was
actually going to marry me, he didn't like it one little
bit!'

'But I don't understand why. You'd left the other
man, hadn't you?'

Her voice bitter, Etta said tersely, 'Of course. Sicilian
men don't marry their mistresses. And for one to marry
someone else's mistress — well, that is a totally unac-
ceptable offence to their moral code. A stigma on the
family name that couldn't be lived down for a couple of
centuries at least.'

CHAPTER FIVE

'YOU can't mean that!' Bryony exclaimed in astonishment.

'You wouldn't think it would matter so much in this day and age, would you?' Etta replied. 'But here it does, especially if it's one of the important families — and a titled one at that.'

'But you said that you met Antonio in Rome. Surely if no one here knew about your past, then. . .' Her voice faded as she looked at Etta's face. 'Rafe told everyone,' she said hollowly.

'Of course. As soon as he realised that he couldn't persuade Antonio to give me up, he let the whole island know about my — my previous connection — and coloured the account quite a bit in the telling,' she added bitterly. 'He hoped that Antonio might be too ashamed to marry me then.' Her face softened and a tender look of remembrance came into her eyes. 'But Tonio needed me, and nothing Rafe could do or say would dissuade him.'

'He must have loved you very much,' Bryony smiled, a wistful note in her voice.

'He came to. But he needed me more. He wasn't very well, you see, and I had been a nurse and knew how to look after him. And I made him laugh, too, so that he began to enjoy life again. And when he was feeling ill I kept Rafe away from him so that he had peace and quiet.'

'I bet Rafe wished that he'd never introduced you to his uncle in the first place,' Bryony remarked.

'Oh, but he did that on purpose, hoping that Antonio would be attracted to me.'

'But I don't understand. How is that possible if he didn't want Antonio to marry you?'

Etta came to sit in the chair beside Bryony and leant towards her, her voice dropping to a confiding note. 'My old lover was an Australian who was working in Rome. His contract was almost over and he was due to go back home. There was no question of my going back to Australia with him, or of him staying on. We'd met Rafe frequently because both men were in the same line of business, so Rafe knew that we were about to part, of course. A week or so before my Australian went home, Rafe gave a small party, as a farewell, he said. Antonio was there. He'd gone to Rome to have some medical treatment.' Her voice hardened. 'Rafe introduced us, making quite sure that Antonio knew about "my position", as Rafe called it.'

'And so making sure that Antonio would never get any ideas about marriage, as he thought,' Bryony guessed.

'Exactly. But Rafe was worried about his uncle and wanted him to have a constant companion who would look after him and nurse him when he was ill. He knew I'd been a nurse and so he decided on me.'

'But why not just hire you as a nurse?'

'Because he knew I wouldn't do it.' Etta shrugged. 'I must admit, Bryony, dear, that I'd got a little too used to the good life to want to go back to nursing.'

'So why not just employ any old nurse?'

'They'd tried that. First with a male nurse whom Antonio couldn't stand, then with a woman who threatened all kind of lawsuits when he made a pass at her.'

Bryony laughed. 'He wasn't all that ill, then?'

'No, he still had his moments,' Etta smiled. 'So Rafe

decided to find him a suitable companion. A nurse-cum-mistress.'

'So he deliberately brought you together?'

'Oh, yes. Rafe never does anything without a reason.'

Bryony thought about that for a minute, then said, 'He must have been really mad when Antonio insisted on marrying you.'

Etta grinned. 'I'll say! He did everything he could to try and dissuade him. But Antonio was tough mentally, even though his body was frail. And he was still the head of the family. In the end he sent Rafe to England for a couple of years.'

'Good for him,' Bryony said warmly. She went to say something else, but hesitated.

'What is it?'

Bryony shook her head. 'It doesn't matter.'

'You're wondering why Antonio was so insistent about marrying me when I was already his mistress,' Etta guessed shrewdly.

'Well — yes.'

'Because he was afraid of losing me, of going back to his old lonely life.'

'Was there a possibility of that?'

'Yes. After my Australian had been home about six months or so his circumstances changed and he wanted me to go out there to join him, with the strong possibility that we would be married. Then Antonio knew that the only way he could keep me was to marry me himself. You see in that time I'd already nursed him back to health; he felt young again and life was not only well worth living, it was worth hanging on to. I like to think that he also wanted to marry me as a return for giving him that.'

The reward for becoming indispensable, the choice of two men who both wanted her, Bryony thought, and tried to push out of her mind her own broken romance. 'But Rafe blamed you, of course,' she said.

'Naturally. And now I don't have Antonio to protect me any more.'

'Well, you don't have to worry about Rafe getting at you through me; I let him know that I was quite definitely on your side. He won't bother with me again.'

Etta gave her a musing look. 'You know, I'm not sure that's altogether a good thing.'

'Why ever not?'

'Well, just as he wanted you to spy on me for him, it would be useful to have someone who knows what *he's* up to.'

Turning quickly to look at her, Bryony said, 'You're not serious?'

'Yes, I am. Think about it, Bryony; Rafe took you into his confidence tonight and he could again. He's obviously attracted to you, too, or he would never have taken you out to dinner. Maybe all that about telling you his side of the story was just an excuse to get you to go with him. I think he's intrigued by you, and your broken romance. Maybe he's even thinking of catching you on the rebound. And you could take advantage of that to get close to him.'

Bryony was staring at her in consternation. 'My God, Etta, do you know what you're saying?'

'Don't think I'm suggesting anything immoral,' Etta said quickly. 'You could go around with him and find things out but still keep him at arm's length. And that in itself would be quite a magnet to him,' Etta added drily. 'Rafe isn't in the habit of having his women play hard to get.'

'He's had plenty of women, then, has he?' Bryony said over-casually.

'My dear! Have you taken a good look at him?'

'He is very attractive, admittedly.'

'And has a reputation as a lover to go with it, by all
accounts. That doesn't always follow, you know.'

'Doesn't it?' Bryony said faintly.

Etta laughed suddenly. 'Don't look so worried, my
dear.'

Bryony rose to her feet. 'I don't have to be; after
tonight he'll never want to see me again, so the possibility doesn't arise.' She bent to kiss Etta's cheek.
'Goodnight. It's been a long day.'

She walked to the door but stopped when Etta said,
'Oh, by the way—how was Etna?'

Bursting into laughter, Bryony said, 'About to
erupt—just like me if I ever have to see Rafe again!'

It rained the next day so she didn't go out, but the
day after that was fine so Bryony continued to get to
know the island by going to Syracuse. The estate car
had been mended so she and Giovanni used that instead
of the Rolls. And Maria came along, too, Etta telling
them all to have a day's holiday before the first guests
arrived. But even though they were in a far less
noticeable car Bryony ducked down as they went
through the village so that no one could report back to
Rafe.

Syracuse was in the opposite direction to Taormina,
but was again on the coast, facing the Ionian Sea. The
old part of the town was on a small island linked to the
main urban area by a couple of bridges. Giovanni
dropped her off there but made it plain that their idea
of a day off was to go to the modern shops and to see a
film, not wander round old churches and ruins. So he
and Maria drove back to the main shopping centre,
leaving Bryony to find the tourist sites on her own. The
day was pleasantly warm and there was lots to see.
Winding streets gave glimpses of beautiful baroque
palaces built of local stone, off-white and mellow. And

in the main square there was a huge cathedral, its columned portico framed against the blue of the sky.

Bryony stood in front of it to admire and take a photograph to send home to her parents, but she couldn't help glancing round to see if a tall figure was watching or walking towards her, just as she'd been glancing round all through her walk. No one came; she was safe from Rafe's importuning. But somehow she felt a strange disappointment that wouldn't go away, however hard she tried to dismiss it.

Having dutifully inspected the interior of the cathedral, an adaptation of an ancient temple dedicated to Minerva, seen the fountain of Arethusa, and admired the view over the harbour, Bryony went into a café and treated herself to a glass of *granita*, an iced coffee flavoured with almond. Sitting alone at her table drinking it, she experienced an intense feeling of loneliness. It was a very new feeling and one she didn't like. Always before there had been someone: her parents, friends, Jeff; and it was strange to feel so lost and alone. I shouldn't need anyone, she thought with annoyance. I'm independent and self-sufficient. But she wouldn't have minded a friend joining her then — even Rafe.

Determinedly shaking off the feeling, Bryony finished her drink and walked briskly back through the town, over the bridge and up the long road leading to the Greek theatre. On the way she cheered herself up by imagining the mathematician Archimedes, who used to live in Syracuse in ancient times, so excited by his discovery of the principle of water displacement that he forgot to put his clothes on after his bath and went running through the streets stark naked, shouting, 'Eureka!' But later he was so absorbed in a mathematical problem when the city was attacked by the Romans that he forgot to run away and was killed by a soldier.

The theatre was the usual semicircular shape with tiers of seats, and again faced the harbour and the sea—or would have done if the Romans hadn't blocked the view with their high background to the stage, and the modern Syracusans hadn't built their new town to obscure it completely. Feeling slightly disappointed, Bryony went to have a look at the *Latomia del Paradiso*, the Paradise Quarry, which her ticket also covered. It turned out to be a magic place; an ancient quarry with vertically steep, very high sides, hung now with trailing plants, and at its foot an overgrown garden of orange trees and oleanders.

Bryony walked along the stony path, empty now because it was siesta time, enjoying the scents of the flowers, then caught her breath as she came out of the garden and found herself at the foot of an immensely high cave, like a great cleft in the rock, which grew narrower at the top. Gazing up in awe-struck wonder, she went nearer and heard her own footsteps echoing as she walked. The inside of the cave was dark after the sun, and she stopped and blinked, waiting until her eyes had adjusted before she went on. And then she heard it—a faint whisper that was picked up by the extraordinary acoustics and thrown back and forth across the cave. 'Bryony! Bryony! Bryony!' The sound rose and fell, rose and fell.

For a few moments she thought that she must have said it herself, but it wasn't her voice; the echo was in the deeper tone of a man. She stood still, looking into the darkness, hearing his footsteps long before Rafe came near enough to the light to be seen.

With laughter in her voice, she said, 'Everyone who comes to Sicily comes to Syracuse——'

'And everyone who comes to Syracuse comes to the quarry.' They finished in unison, their voices vibrating from the walls, from the roof, from the floor, swirling around them.

Rafe laughed and took her arm. 'Let's get out of here.'

'Out of here — here — here,' the echo called after him in regret.

They didn't speak again until they were in the garden. Looking back at the cave, Bryony said, 'What an extraordinary place.'

'That's what you said about the hotel in Taormina.'

'Yes, but that was man-made; this is a natural phenomenon.'

Rafe shook his head. 'No, you're wrong. There are several quarries like this around the town. They were used to provide the stone to build the ancient city, and when the Syracusans were at war they kept their captives imprisoned here.'

'But the cave; that surely must be natural?'

'No.' Again he shook his head. 'No one really knows why it was built like that, although there is a legend that the tyrant Dionysius kept his prisoners in the cave, and because of the acoustics could listen to their conversations. To see if they were plotting against him, I suppose. That's why they call the cave the Ear of Dionysius.'

'It even looks a bit like the shape of an earlobe.'

'So it does.'

Something in his tone made Bryony glance quickly at Rafe to see if he was mocking her, but found his eyes fixed on her with a contemplative look in them. 'You've seen and talked about all this many times before,' she said lightly.

'Quite a few.'

'Does it always work — saying the girl's name so that it echoes through the cave?'

'I suppose that rather depends on what you mean by "work",' Rafe answered, in no way put out.

'Well, I suppose that rather depends on what you want.' She reached up to pick a sweet-smelling blossom from a tree. 'How did you find me this time? Have you got spies here, as well as everywhere else on the island?'

'I'm flattered that you think me so omniscient. No, I found out much more easily.'

'How?'

'I rang the villa and asked for you. Etta answered and she told me where you were.'

'Did she, indeed?' Bryony said tartly.

'That's what I thought,' Rafe agreed. 'Do you think she *wants* to throw us together?'

Now who's being blunt? Bryony thought indignantly, and silently cursed Etta. But she tossed her head and met his challenge head-on. 'Why on earth should she?'

'Oh, I can think of several reasons,' Rafe answered with a ghost of a smile.

'Well, I can't — and I can't think of any reason why you should want to see me again, either, if it comes to that,' Bryony said, unable to resist throwing in her own challenge.

Putting a hand under her elbow, Rafe began to walk back with her up the slope to the entrance. 'For one thing, you seem to need a guide to tell you all about these ancient places.'

'If I wanted a guide I could join a tour,' she pointed out.

'So why don't you?'

'Maybe I will.'

'No, you won't,' Rafe said confidently. 'You like to be alone to soak up the history of the place. You want the stones to speak to you, but how can they do that when you're with a crowd of people, with a guide who shouts the facts at you as fast as she can so that she can hurry you all on to the next place? You are definitely not that kind of tourist, Bryony.'

Which was true, but then she hadn't enjoyed being entirely alone, either. 'Do you make a habit of reading characters?' she asked him lightly. 'Or is it just that mine is so transparent?'

'Don't you like me being able to see what you are like?'

'Me — or all women?'

'Ah, now I understand.' He gave her an amused smile. 'Etta has obviously been — poisoning your ears.' He nodded, pleased he'd found the phrase he was looking for. 'What has she been saying about me?'

'Can't you guess?'

'Do you want me to do a smear campaign against myself? Give you a list of all my faults?'

'Well, at least you admit you have some,' she told him, unable to resist a mischievous smile.

'You have trapped me,' he laughed. 'Of course I have faults. Doesn't everyone?'

She shrugged. 'I suppose so.'

'For example I find that I am completely unable to resist beautiful girls with ash-blonde hair and grey eyes.'

Bryony wrinkled her nose. 'What a line!'

Rafe threw up his hands in despair and became very Italian. 'You Englishwomen! You're hopeless. I give up. All right, Bryony, what would you like to see now? The Street of the Tombs? The Catacombs?'

She had stopped to look at him and burst into laughter. 'Am I really as bad as that?'

'Worse. I don't know why I want to be with you,' he said in mock-despair.

'Nor do I.'

His eyes suddenly intent, Rafe said, 'But I have already told you.' But before she could do more than blink he had taken her hand to guide her across the road. 'Come on, we'll go and have some lunch.'

'I was going to skip lunch,' she said mildly, after he'd walked her to a nearby restaurant and they were sitting down.

'You can skip meals in England; in Sicily the food is too good.'

That made her laugh again. 'Don't you have anything good to say about England?'

'Many things — but you don't like compliments,' he said with a smile.

Bryony began to see even more reasons why he had such a reputation with women. I must be careful, she thought; Rafe is far too experienced at this game for me to handle. But it was nice to be with a man again, especially such a good-looking one, a man who caught the eyes of all the women they'd passed in the street. And it was nice to be flattered even though she knew that was all it was. She would have liked to know just why he had singled her out but knew she wouldn't find out unless he chose to tell her — or until he'd achieved his purpose. He would just fob her off with compliments that she didn't believe, and implications that he made all too easy to believe. Watching him as he read through the menu, she realised how diabolically clever he was at handling women. It would be an easy thing to fall for him, especially for a woman like herself, on the rebound from another romance. The bitterly triumphant 'I'll show him!' feeling came into it, a need to make the old lover jealous, and also a desperate need to know that you were still attractive to men. In those circumstances, and with a man as gorgeously masculine as Rafe, what girl could possibly resist him?

'You're not reading your menu,' Rafe complained, cutting into her thoughts. 'And you are looking at me with eyes as cold as a statue's. What are you thinking?'

'About England.'

'The English climate would make anyone feel cold,'

he agreed. 'But was it just of England that you were thinking?'

'What do you mean?'

'Perhaps you were thinking of your—friends at home.'

'Why should I think of my friends?'

Stretching out his hand, Rafe let his finger run down the length of hers as it lay on the table. 'It would be very strange if a girl as beautiful as you did not have a boyfriend at home.'

'Oh, a boyfriend. I've hundreds of those.'

His eyes shot up to meet hers, then creased into a grin. 'I meant a special boyfriend, someone you love.'

'No,' she said coolly. 'I have no one like that.'

'Not now, perhaps, but in the past?'

Her chin came up. 'Of course. Dozens. How about you? Do you have a special girlfriend?'

Rafe shook his head, his eyes amused at her taking the conversation into her own hands. 'No.'

'You mean not at the moment, do you? But obviously plenty of women in the past.'

His eyebrows rose. 'Obviously?'

'Oh, yes, I think so.' She picked up the menu. 'I'll have the antipasto and grilled scampi, please.'

Reaching over, he plucked the menu from her hands. 'You shall have anything you wish, but first you are going to explain to me what you mean by that word "obviously". I do not think I like it.'

Deciding to pay him back in kind, Bryony opened her eyes wide and said in a voice husky with awe, 'But Rafe, you're so handsome and charming. I've never known a man as attractive to women as you. Why, just look at the way they all stare at you in the street. You must have girls who'd give *anything* to be with you,' slightly stressing the 'anything'. 'And here you are wining and dining little old me,' she added in fulsome tones.

For a long moment Rafe didn't speak, just sat looking at her with features set into an unreadable mask. Then his mouth twisted a little. 'I beg your pardon; I have *obviously* angered you by my obviousness — is that what you are trying to say?'

Immediately she felt a fool and her cheeks flushed, until she realised that it was Rafe who had been supposed to feel a fool but he had turned the tables on her by making her feel unfair. How clever he is, she thought, and remembered Etta telling her that he never did anything without a reason. Anger and resentment stirred within her. Why can't everything be straight-forward? she thought bitterly. I hate being devious — and even more I hate men who are devious. Lifting her chin, she said curtly, 'Yes.'

Rafe gave her a surprised glance, then laughed. 'I cannot win with you, can I? Tell me, what must I do to please you?'

'Why do you want to please me?' she countered.

'Well, now, I must not pay you even the smallest compliment, so what must I say? That I want you to spy on Etta for me — you would believe that, would you not? What else?' He put his arm on the table and rested his chin on it, pretending to muse. 'I have it!' He pointed his finger at her. 'I want you to poison Etta, and let's say Maria and Giovanni as well, so that I can move into the villa. You would certainly believe that of me. Yes, you would much prefer to think bad of me than good.'

Bryony's face had tightened but she looked steadily into his eyes. 'I have heard nothing but bad of you,' she pointed out.

'Has Etta nothing good to say of me, then?' he asked harshly.

'No, but then you have only yourself to thank.'

He gave her a glittering look. 'For any particular reason?'

'She told me you let everyone here know about her past.'

'About her lovers, you mean?' he said bluntly.

Bryony gave him a wary look. 'About the Australian, yes.'

'That was all she told you?' He gave a shrug, saying nothing, but implying a lot.

'Were there other men, then?'

'That you must ask Etta.'

'Even so, it was hardly kind of you to tell everyone here about it. You tried everything you could to stop your uncle marrying her, didn't you?'

'Yes, I admit it.'

She gave a little gasp at his openness. Anger rose in her and she said forcefully, 'So that you wouldn't lose the villa. Or was it because you were jealous? Were you so insecure that you didn't want to share your uncle, share his love?'

Rafe's eyes glinted but before he could reply the waiter came to take their order. When he'd given it he said, 'Did Etta accuse me of that, too?'

'No, she didn't. But she would have had every right to. OK, maybe there have been other men in her past, but what else could you expect at her age? But she did her best to make Antonio happy. She was very fond of him and very upset when he died. And now she's alone. A widow in a foreign country. And as Antonio's nearest relative you ought to be looking after her, not making her life a misery.'

'Well, she has certainly won your sympathy,' Rafe commented shortly. 'Whether she truly deserves it or not.'

She gave him a fulminating look. 'You're always

making obscure remarks like that. Trying to make me
unsure about Etta. Well, I'm not. I believe every word
she says about you.'

'Then nothing I can possibly say will make you
change your mind, so we might as well completely
forget about it and enjoy our lunch,' Rafe returned
calmly.

Still angry, Bryony said shortly, 'I don't know what
I'm doing here. Whenever I'm with you we fight like
cat and dog.'

An amused look came into Rafe's eyes. 'But you are
here with me,' he pointed out.

'Yes.' Her expression softened a little but there was
a note almost of bewilderment in her voice. 'So I am.'

Their food came but Bryony couldn't enjoy it. Rafe
tried to draw her into conversation, but she answered
him distractedly, as if her thoughts were elsewhere. In
reality they were entirely on him, and on her own
vulnerability where he was concerned. It came to her
suddenly that she was arguing against him and accusing
him so vehemently because she was afraid of falling for
him. Falling for him badly. But she didn't want another
relationship, another affair. And she definitely didn't
want to get hurt again. She gave him a nervous glance,
her eyes confused. She hardly knew him and all that
she had heard was bad. I should despise him, she
thought. But I don't. I can't. No matter that I know
how cruel he has been to Etta. Why, he's even admitted
that himself. But I just can't hate him. And today I was
glad to see him, really glad. When I saw him walking
towards me out of the darkness in the cave I could have
run to him.

She had given up all pretence of eating and was
staring down at her plate.

'What is it, Bryony?' Rafe's voice cut into her

thoughts and she gave him a tremulous, almost frightened glance. 'Don't you like it?'

'Oh, no, it—it's fine. I did tell you I wasn't very hungry. I'm sorry.'

'Would you like something else?'

She shook her head. 'No, thanks.'

'Very well.' Lifting his hand, he called for the bill.

When they were outside on the pavement, she said, 'I'm sorry, I ruined your lunch.'

'Yes,' he agreed. 'But I think I will forgive you. What would you like to do now?'

But Bryony had made up her mind. 'There isn't time for anything. I have to meet Maria and Giovanni shortly.'

He didn't believe her; she hadn't really expected him to, but he didn't argue. Giving her a quizzical look, Rafe merely said, 'Perhaps we could arrange to go sightseeing together next time. Then I wouldn't have to try and find you. When would you like to go?'

'I'm sorry,' Bryony answered jerkily. 'Etta has some friends coming over tomorrow and I'll be going around with them.'

He lifted a questioning eyebrow. 'Some English friends?'

'No, American.'

'How long will they be staying?'

'I'm not sure,' she prevaricated, not wanting him to tie her down. 'At least a couple of weeks.'

'But you surely won't wish to be with them every day. Will you promise to telephone me when you are free?'

Taking a deep breath, Bryony said a firm, 'No.'

Tilting his head a little, Rafe raised an eyebrow. 'That was a very definite refusal.'

'It was meant to be. I don't want to see you again, Rafe.'

'You've said that before,' he reminded her.

Trying to forget that she had been just as determined last time, she said, 'Well, now I really mean it. It would be — disloyal to Etta for me to see you again.'

'Even though she told me where to find you today?'

She winced. 'When we meet all we do is argue. That isn't what I came here for.'

'So why did you come to Sicily?'

'For a holiday, of course.' But she said it too quickly and had the feeling that, again, he didn't believe her.

'Couldn't we agree not to argue?'

She gave a rueful smile. 'Somehow I don't think we'd keep to it.' Lifting her head, she said, 'Let's face it, Rafe, we just rub each other up the wrong way the whole time. I don't trust you and I don't like ——'

Reaching out, he put a long finger on her lips, silencing her. 'Don't say you don't like me, Bryony, because I know you do. You're just afraid to admit it. Afraid of trusting your heart again.' Gently he ran his fingertip over her lips, the light touch a scintillating caress. 'But we will see each other again — it's inevitable.' For a long moment his eyes continued to hold hers and she really thought that he was going to kiss her again, but then he straightened abruptly, gave her his usual small bow, and said, '*Ciao*, Bryony,' before he walked away.

There were hours yet before the time that she had actually arranged to meet the others, but Bryony could find no enthusiasm now to visit any more tourist sites. She walked to the nearest piazza and sat on a wooden bench, gazing unseeingly at the passing scene. She tried to tell herself that she had done the right thing, that Rafe had no real interest in her and was either just amusing himself or playing some deeper game she couldn't fathom. She was also shocked by her own deepening attraction to him. She had just broken off one affair, so how could she possibly be attracted to anyone else in so short a time? But one thing was for sure; her unhappiness at not being with Jeff had entirely gone. She could think of him now without a pang, with almost a feeling of relief that it was over.

But she wasn't free. Rafe had somehow reversed her initial feelings of dislike into attraction, into physical awareness. And he knew it, too, damn him! She'd behaved like a—a mindless idiot back there in the restaurant. She should have kept it light, not let him see that he'd got to her. But the revelation had come as too much of a surprise for her to conceal it.

A young man came up to her and began to speak, but received such a freezing look that he broke off and went on his way. Men! she thought with fury. All they think of is sex. But then Bryony gave an inner, reluctant laugh as she realised that it wasn't far from her own mind right now, either.

This wouldn't do. Getting briskly to her feet, she strode away from the bench towards the Roman amphitheatre. The young men in Sicily were far too virile for a girl to sit alone for too long.

Etta's American guests arrived the next day; they were three youngish middle-aged couples who were used to living at a high standard and at a fairly fast pace, even though they said they had come to Sicily for a rest. Giovanni went to pick them up in the Rolls, but there wasn't enough space for all their luggage so it followed behind in a taxi. They were tired after their flight and wanted only to have a restful evening, and to lounge around the pool and to stroll in the garden the next day. Bryony kept largely out of their way, but the following morning they were eager to go out sightseeing. They had hired a Cadillac limo, big enough to take all six of them, and a guide and driver, and it was fitted with a fridge, television and video. The driver, Stefano, spoke a little English, but not enough to act as a guide or have a conversation with the guests. The limo was his best car, his pride and joy, which he allowed no one else to drive.

Bryony sat next to Stefano in the front, grateful that the Americans had accepted her suggestion that they go first to see Mount Etna. Fortunately they were easygoing people, willing to be pleased by all they saw, and not too deeply concerned about every detail of the island's history. So Bryony got away with her first day as a guide quite credibly.

Her life, though, became very busy, as she shopped, cooked, and took the guests out almost every other day. Having been to so few places, she had to spend hours of her so-called leisure time reading up on the places they were to visit the next day, but luckily Stefano knew the island like the seamed palm of his hand and she was able to learn a lot from him. She bought a video cassette of the island which she watched on the car's video while the guests were having lunch one day, and was still watching it when they returned. They set off to the next place, Stefano carefully choosing a route through pretty scenery, and Bryony was stunned to look over her shoulder to find that the Americans had put on the video themselves and were engrossed in watching it while they were driving along.

But their hard work to make the Americans' stay a happy one paid off because they enjoyed themselves so much that they rang some friends who flew out to join them for the last couple of days and stayed on for another week. The original three couples left, promising to recommend the villa to all of their friends, and Etta's contacts brought the promise of more guests, making Bryony say cautiously, 'It looks as if we might be successful.'

'Of course we are,' Etta answered positively. 'With you as the chef and guide, how could we possibly fail?'

But Bryony knew their success was largely due to Etta. She came into her own as a hostess, her warm personality making the guests feel immediately at home, and her vivacity and gift for telling a good anecdote keeping them amused over dinner and the evening bridge tables.

Rafe made no attempt to contact her during those weeks and she didn't expect him to, but she had no doubt that he was well aware of what she was doing. It was the strangest thing; Bryony had been in love with Jeff for nearly two years and had been as close to him as it was possible to be to a man, but now, in the moments when she had time to be alone and think, it was never to him that her thoughts strayed. Always it was to Rafe, with a sense of loss for his disturbing presence. Determinedly, then, Bryony would force her mind on to other things. Rafe was not for her; to think of him was crazy, almost as crazy as letting her attraction for him develop into somethig deeper would have been. An affair with him, although she strongly suspected it would have been physically out of this world, would have led to nothing but hurt and humiliation. So Bryony concentrated on her cooking and the next guided tour, but at night she had no control over her subconscious and couldn't shut out the lean face and intent eyes that came to haunt her dreams.

It was almost a month since she had last seen him before she even heard his name again, and then Etta, one morning, opened her post and looked up to say shortly, 'Rafe's back.'

'Back? Has he been away?' Bryony tried to keep her tone casual.

'So he says. For the last two weeks. I wonder where he went? To Rome on business, I suppose.'

'I'm surprised he's bothered to let you know he's back in Sicily,' Bryony remarked carefully.

'Well, I don't suppose he would have done, but he's written to ask if he can keep his boat at the jetty now that the weather is warm enough to sail again.'

'Is that where he usually keeps it?'

'Yes. He has a small yacht that used to belong to Antonio, and a motorboat that he bought himself. He takes them out of the water in the winter, of course, and keeps them in a boatyard in Catania. But in the past he's always kept the yacht at the jetty in the summer.' She looked broodingly down at the letter. 'I'm not sure that I ought to let him use the jetty; it might be the thin end of the wedge. Why can't he keep it at the marina with the motorboat?'

Her heart thumping a little, Bryony said, 'Would it mean him coming to the house? You don't want that.'

'No, I certainly don't,' Etta agreed. 'He might find out about our guests. But there again. . .' she hesitated '. . . I don't want to give Rafe any excuse to go around telling people that I've banned him from the place completely. Maybe I'll phone him about it.'

The two women had got into the habit of having a quiet period together after dinner, in the room they had made into an office, when the guests were having their coffee. It was a time when they could discuss any changes they needed to make, groceries they needed to buy, and the hundred and one other things that went into running an establishment like the hotel. Tonight Bryony waited eagerly for Etta to arrive, not really knowing what she wanted the older woman to say. She didn't want to see Rafe again, of course, and yet. . . But if he came to the villa to reach his boat, then she might have to. He might seek her out again. So what if he did? she asked herself sternly. Nothing's changed.

Not that he was likely to, not when a whole month had gone by without a word. Still, he had been away. . .

Etta breezed into the room and sank into an armchair. 'Strong and black, please,' she ordered.

Smiling, Bryony poured out the coffee she had brought with her on a tray. 'Difficult, were they?'

'That American who's by himself thinks he knows everything. We had quite an argument over——' She broke off to take the coffee. 'But it doesn't matter. I suppose when people are paying they think it's OK to argue with one's hostess. How has your day been, Bryony, dear?'

'Fine. Everything's going smoothly. I shall need a girl from the village to help me on Saturday, though, because it's Maria's and Giovanni's weekend off.'

They discussed the subject for a few minutes, then Etta said, 'I rang Rafe. We've reached a compromise. I've said that he can moor his boat at the jetty so long as he repairs the chapel roof and only comes out to the jetty by motorboat. That way he won't come near the house.'

'You certainly seem to have got the better of that deal. When is he bringing it?' Bryony asked lightly.

'I've no idea. Quite soon, I should imagine.'

Bryony's room overlooked the bay and she found that, when she went to bed around midnight, she could just glimpse the end of the jetty if she stood on the tapestry stool that was by her bed. The moon was almost full and the dark shadow of the wooden pier stood out against the silvery waves. That night, and for the next three nights, there was just the square mass of the pier, but on Saturday, when the moon was almost full, she looked out and saw the graceful curves of a boat, its mast gently dipping with the rippling waves. For a few moments she stood transfixed, her mind not consciously working, then she turned and ran down the

back stairs, letting herself out of a side-door and
running across the sweetly scented garden towards the
sound of the sea.

He was waiting for her at the end of the jetty, leaning
against a post, his silhouette outlined in the moonlight.
He heard her coming and straightened up. She stopped
a few yards from him, suddenly uncertain. For a few
moments they faced each other across the sand, but
then Rafe strode to her, swung her up in his arms and
carried her along the jetty and aboard the boat. In the
cabin he set her down, then slowly, deliberately, he
began to undress her.

CHAPTER SIX

A GREAT roaring tidal wave lifted her to its crest, held her there as it crashed and whirled around her. Bryony cried out, her mind suspended as her body arched in one long, exquisite peak of pleasure. Only afterwards, when her cry had turned to a sighing moan, did Rafe cease to hold back and let himself reach his own groaning climax.

Bryony lay in his arms, her body quivering, her breathing short and unsteady. Slowly she opened her eyes, became aware of the dimly lit cabin and the berth on which they lay, so narrow that Rafe had hardly room to lie beside her. There were beads of sweat on his brow and around his parted mouth and the slumberous look of satiation in his eyes. Seeing her looking at him, he put his hand against her face and bent to kiss her gently.

'You were wonderful, *cara*. And so beautiful, so lovely.'

His hand slid down the length of her body in a long caress, no longer exploring, no longer seeking to arouse her to the height of sexual desire. Bryony smiled. 'You were pretty good yourself.'

Lifting himself on to his elbow, Rafe looked down at her and laughed. 'Coming from an English girl, I shall take that as a great compliment.'

She ran her fingertips over his broad chest, doing her own exploring, as there had been no time to do before, but he took her hand and kissed each finger in turn. 'I was afraid you wouldn't come down to the beach,' he told her.

She shook her head. 'No, you weren't. You knew that I'd come. That's why you wrote to Etta and brought the boat here.'

His mouth twisted a little. 'I certainly hoped that you would. I wanted you so much, my sweet Bryony. From the moment that you slapped my face in the cellar.'

Her eyebrows rose in surprise. 'You kissed me before I slapped you,' she pointed out.

'Ah, yes, but that was. . .' He shrugged with one shoulder. 'What shall I call it?'

'A pass,' Bryony supplied wryly.

Rafe grinned. 'Yes, a pass. To see how you would react.'

'And?'

'And you instinctively slapped my face, so I had to revise my opinion of you.'

Her eyes filled with curiosity. 'You'd already formed one? What was it?'

He looked at her for a moment, then shook his head. 'Perhaps I will tell you some other time. Not now, *mia cara*, not now. All I want now is to look at your beautiful body, and to kiss you like this, and like this.'

Reputation hadn't lied; he was a terrific lover, giving almost more than he took, always putting her pleasure before his own. He made the act beautiful, a thing of grace and wonder, revealing pleasures she had never known existed. She didn't feel at all used, as she had often done with Jeff, when he had taken his own pleasure and then rolled over to fall immediately asleep. Rafe made her feel as if her body and its sensations were the most important things in the world, to be idolised and treasured. She felt like an instrument on which he played the most marvellous music, evoked the most glorious of symphonies. And Bryony responded eagerly to his touch, delighting in the giving of her body, hearing with satisfaction his shuddering groans as he reached his own peak of excitement again and yet again.

It was almost five in the morning before they came out of the cabin, and already the dawn was breaking. There was a breeze coming from the sea and the air felt cold and damp. Bryony shivered, rubbing her arms, and Rafe took a jacket from the back of the cabin door, kissing her as she slid her arms into the sleeves. He walked her slowly back through the garden to the villa, the dew wet on the grass. It was dark and she stumbled a little, but he held her within the strength of his arm, and at the door he kissed her again, his lips hard and possessive now. 'When the flag is flying at the top of the mast,' he told her, 'then you'll know I'm aboard. Come to me if you can.'

She nodded, her mind still dizzy and satiated by love. 'Yes, all right. Rafe. . .' She put her hand on his shoulder, wanting to thank him for tonight, but not knowing how. To just say the words would have been wrong somehow, for her feelings went much deeper than a formal offer of gratitude could describe.

But he understood; taking her hand, he turned it over to lightly kiss the palm, a gesture that claimed their new intimacy, claimed her as his own. 'Goodnight, *cara*,' he said softly.

He waited while she went inside, closing and locking the door as quietly as possible, then slipped up the back stairs to her room. Only then did she realise she was still wearing his jacket, but she was glad; it was a part of him that she could keep for a while along with the remembrance of tonight. Going to the window, she looked out and saw Rafe's darker shadow against the greying light. He lifted a hand in farewell and ran back across the garden, and presently, as she undressed, Bryony heard the throb of an engine as the motorboat left to go back to Catania. She stood still for a long

moment, remembering, then moved to stand in front of
the long mirror on the wardrobe door. I have a new
lover, she thought. And such a lover! Never had her
body felt so alive, so *feminine*. Putting her hands on her
shoulders, she ran them down over her naked skin,
feeling its silkiness as Rafe must have felt it.

Her eyes in the mirror were enormous pools of
awakened sensuality. She knew now what love could be
like, what it should be like. With Jeff it had been just a
pleasurable act, although not always exciting, sometimes just accommodating. But tonight Rafe had taught
her the beauty of love and of her own body. He had
given her the gift of his expertise and skill to lift her
into this brilliant new world where anything less would
be— Her thoughts broke off and Bryony frowned at
her reflection.

Skill and expertise. The words stuck in her mind.
Was that all it had been for Rafe? Not spontaneity, not
the overpowering desire that had drawn her irresistibly
down to the beach to meet him? He had said that he
wanted her but there had been no urgency in his taking
of her, no primitive, wild abandon in his lovemaking.
Instead there had been deliberateness, in the way he
had written to Etta about the boat, in the way he had
waited until today to bring it to the bay, probably
knowing that Maria and Giovanni would be away and
it would be safe for her to sneak through the house.

A sudden shiver ran through her and Bryony quickly
picked up Rafe's jacket and pulled it on, holding the
collar close against her face, smelling the faint traces of
his musky aftershave, and a more delicate aroma. She
tried to regain her earlier euphoric mood but it wouldn't
come back and she lifted a vulnerable, staring gaze to
the mirror. 'Sicilian men don't marry their mistresses'.
The words echoed through her mind. She remembered,
too, that she had suspected Rafe of some deeper game.

Was this a part of it? Had she become his pawn, to
manipulate and use against Etta? Had he made her fall
in love with him just so——? Again her thoughts
screeched to a halt. In love? Is that what I am? Or is it
just my body that's in love with what he does to me,
that craves the fulfilment that only he can give?

Oh, God, she thought, don't let me fall in love with
him. Please, not with him. But hadn't it been love that
had taken her to him? What else could have drawn her
like a magnet to that most wonderful of nights? The
night of my nights, she thought with almost humble
awe. And what if I am in love? Wasn't it possible for
Rafe to feel the same way about her? Maybe it wasn't
a game. Maybe it wasn't even just sex. Couldn't he
have felt the same attraction she did? After all, he had
gone out of his way to find her and. . . Her hands had
gone into the pockets of the jacket and found something
in the right one, something metallic. Slowly, with a
strange reluctance, Bryony pulled it out and held it on
the palm of her hand. It was a bracelet, a pretty gold
one about an inch thick. But the clasp was broken and
it wouldn't close. Whoever it belonged to, whichever of
Rafe's women, must have slipped it into the pocket of
the jacket and then forgotten it. But then who wouldn't
forget when being made love to so expertly by Rafe?

With a sudden shudder, Bryony thrust the bracelet
back in the pocket and threw off the jacket, then ran to
pull on her nightdress and get into bed, pulling the
covers up close to her chin, huddled into a ball like a
frightened child. Her body felt so tired, spent, but her
mind wouldn't let her relax, going over and over her
doubts and self-recriminations, and it was fully morning
before she fell asleep.

'Bryony, Bryony, dear, are you all right?'

Etta's voice and the knocking on her door dragged
her reluctantly back to consciousness only a couple of

hours later. She called out and Etta put her head round the door and then came in the room.

'Are you all right, Bryony? It's very late.'

'Is it?' She sat up and groped for the clock on the bedside cabinet. 'I'm sorry, I must have overslept.'

'Didn't you set your alarm?'

'I must have forgotten. Are they all waiting for breakfast? I'll get up now.'

But Etta gave her a searching look. 'Are you sure you're feeling OK, Bryony? You look very heavy-eyed.'

'I couldn't get to sleep last night,' Bryony explained truthfully. 'I'm sorry.'

'It's all right. Only the American who's by himself got up early so I did his breakfast; the others are all having a lie-in. But Mrs Brewster asked for breakfast to be served in her room at nine.' She gave Bryony another close look. 'If you're not feeling well. . .'

'No, I'm fine, really. I'll be right down.'

'I'll leave you to get dressed, then.'

Bryony was almost grateful that she had to rush; it gave her no time to think about last night until much later in the morning. The breakfasts were over, the kitchen cleared, and she was making the beds in the guest rooms, which all faced the sea. Passing a window, she stopped to look at the beach. The yacht was still there, tied to the jetty, but there was no flag flying at the mast. In the bright light of day it seemed almost impossible for last night to have happened. Perhaps it had all been a dream, a dream that had come to her because she had seen the boat. But her tiredness and the stiffness of her body confirmed its reality. Quickly she turned away to finish her task, and when Etta came to find her and tell her the guests wanted to go to Taormina she thankfully went along as their guide.

Rafe didn't phone her but two days later a package

arrived for her in the mail. Bryony took it from Maria without surprise — her parents were always sending her things — but then she saw that it had an Italian stamp and was addressed in writing she didn't recognise. Quickly she ran up to her bedroom, but her fingers slowed as she unwrapped the package, revealing a small jeweller's box. Almost reluctantly she opened it and found inside an exquisite pair of gold earrings. There was a card with it and a very brief note. 'To say thank you for the most wonderful night'. And it was just signed, 'R'.

Bryony closed the case and hurled it across the room, filled with sudden bitter fury. What the hell did he think she was? Some cheap slut who had to be paid in presents, for God's sake? Well, maybe that was exactly what he thought her, she realised with a sob. She had gone to him willingly enough, had put up no resistance when he had started to make love to her. With sickening self-revulsion she remembered Etta's maxim about Rafe only being intrigued if he found her hard to get. Well, she certainly hadn't been that, Bryony thought miserably. And was this the pay-off, this pretty, dutiful bauble? Had he tired of her already, after just one night? Or did he expect her to like it, to be grateful? Just as the other woman he'd given the bracelet to had probably been grateful.

Picking up the box and the jacket from where it was still lying on the floor in the corner where she had flung it, she ran down to the office and wrapped them all into another parcel, taping the bracelet to the earrings box so that he would be sure to see it. She had to look in Etta's address book to find where he lived. She didn't even know that about him! With an unsteady hand she wrote in the address, stuck on some stamps, and walked briskly down to the village to post it, not wanting anyone else at the villa to see.

That evening the phone rang and Etta answered it. 'Rafe! What a surprise. Yes, I'm fine, thank you. Yes, Bryony is fine, too.' She listened, said yes a couple more times and then put down the phone. 'That was Rafe. He's sending some workmen down to repair the chapel roof on Monday.'

It had been an excuse to call, Bryony knew; he had hoped that she would pick up the phone so that she could thank him for his gift, she supposed. Well, he would get it back shortly and then he would know just what she thought of it, and of him.

On Friday night when she looked out Bryony saw a small flag at the top of the boat's mast, and the motorboat tied up alongside. Anger filled her heart; he would have got the earrings back by now so would know that she had found the bracelet and wouldn't want to see him again, but he had still come back, confident that he had only to touch her to win her round. Which was probably true, she admitted to herself with a groan, because she longed to go to him; her body yearned for him to make love to her again. It took all her will-power to switch on the light in her room and stand silhouetted against it for several minutes, wanting Rafe to be sure that she had seen him. Then she firmly drew the curtains and got into bed, reading a book to try and take her mind off him, but completely unable to concentrate. Would he have gone back to Catania yet? Or was he so confident of his own powers that he was still waiting? Unable to bear it any longer, Bryony switched off the light, got out of bed and pushed the curtain aside a fraction to look out. But there was no moon tonight and there was nothing but blackness outside, the land merging with the sea and the sky, so that she couldn't tell whether Rafe was still there or not.

The next morning she kept herself very busy, refusing

to look out at the beach as she went about her daily routine. It was Etta, when they sat down to have a coffee together, who said, 'I see Rafe is working on his boat this morning; getting it ready for the summer, I suppose.'

'It feels like summer now,' Bryony remarked, hoping to divert her. 'It must be almost eighty.'

'You must get out and sunbathe. You're looking very pale again today. I hope I'm not working you too hard, dear.'

'Of course not. I enjoy it, you know that.'

'Well, I'm not so sure. You haven't looked well for the past week. You ought to get out more and meet people. I know!' She gave a delighted smile. 'I've been invited to a charity lunch at the Catania Sheraton next week; you must come along too. And we'll go into town and I'll buy you a new outfit to wear to the party.'

'You don't have to do that, Etta. I can afford one out of my wages.'

'No, I want to buy you a present. It will be fun to help you choose. The guests are still out; let's go now.'

Bryony was more than happy to fall in with that suggestion; the more distance she put between herself and Rafe's disturbing presence the better. Trying as much as possible to put him out of her mind, she entered into Etta's obvious enjoyment of shopping. They went into several high-class boutiques that sold the most gorgeous clothes, all Italian, all beautifully made and designed. The exercise she got working at the villa had made her lose weight and Bryony was able to pick out a suit with a short skirt and sleeveless blouson jacket in a rich tan colour, and the most delicate cream, full-sleeved shirt with a huge lace collar to go under it. The high-heeled shoes to go with it Bryony insisted on buying herself.

The expedition took her mind off Rafe and the two

women enjoyed themselves, Etta also buying herself a
new dress, and it was easy for Bryony to pretend to be
happy as they drove back in the car with all their
packages. But when they reached the villa Maria told
them that Rafe had been up to the house. 'He came for
some water for his engine. I do not know the word in
English — *l'acqua distillata*.'

'Distilled water,' Bryony translated, her throat dry.

'I do not know where Giovanni keeps it, so he went
to look himself in the garage.'

'He wasn't there as we passed.' Dropping her parcels
on the hall table, Etta quickly walked through to the
terrace with Bryony close behind her.

With relief they saw that Rafe was back on his boat,
but he was standing on the deck and was with another
man.

'Oh, no!' Etta exclaimed. 'That's John Cornell, the
American, he's talking to. I thought he'd gone out for
the day. Damn, I knew I shouldn't have let Rafe bring
his boat here.' She turned to Bryony. 'Run down there
quickly and tell Mr Cornell that — that there's a telephone call for him or something.'

'No!'

'What?' Etta stared at her in astonishment.

'You'll have to go. I can't — I don't. . . I don't feel
well,' Bryony muttered desperately, and ran for the
stairs.

From the landing window she watched as Etta walked
down through the garden, stood at the top of the path
leading down to the beach and called out to the hotel
guest. Mr Cornell turned reluctantly but stepped off the
boat and walked towards her. Rafe watched him go but
it was impossible from this distance to see his
expression. Then he lifted his head to look at the villa
and Bryony shot back from the window, afraid that he
might see her. Etta must either have thought up a really

good excuse or exerted all her charm, because Mr Cornell didn't go out again, and presently Rafe cast off the mooring ropes and took the yacht out to sea.

He came back with the sunset but didn't stay on board for another night. Bryony heard the motorboat's engine roaring away as she was cooking dinner. He must have a date tonight, she thought. Maybe he's meeting another of his women. And, masochistically, she wondered where she appeared on his list. What would he give me? Six out of ten. I'm really not that experienced. Or maybe I'll go a point higher because of novelty value.

'Bryony?' Maria touched her arm. 'Are you ill again?'

She managed to smile. 'No, I'm fine.' Her sudden illness she had shrugged off as a stomach cramp and had resisted Etta's offer to take the rest of the day off and go to bed with a hot-water bottle.

Etta was late coming to the office after dinner that evening, and when she did her face was a little flushed. Bryony looked at her with foreboding. 'Did Mr Cornell tell Rafe this is a hotel?'

'I don't think so.' Etta subsided into her usual armchair. 'I tried, of course, but it was difficult to find out without coming right out and asking. It seems that John—Mr Cornell—has his own boat in California, so they were mostly discussing sailing.' She gave an unhappy sigh. 'He might have let it slip, though, and Rafe would be sure to notice. You know how quick he is.'

'Well, at least Mr Cornell is leaving tomorrow so there won't be any more discussions on the yacht.'

To her surprise Etta lifted a hand to pat her hair, a gesture she usually only made when she was feeling feminine. 'As a matter of fact he likes it here so much that he's decided to stay on.'

'Really? How long for?'

'At least a week.'

'Well, that presents no problem as far as accommodation goes, but you'll have to be sure to keep him away from the jetty if Rafe comes back.' Not that she expected him to come back, not now. Even he would have realised that there was no way she was ever going to see him again.

But on Monday morning the workmen arrived to repair the chapel roof and Rafe came with them. She had no warning as she came down the stairs carrying the breakfast tray from Mrs Brewster's room and he walked into the hall when Giovanni opened the door. Bryony came to a sudden stop, her face losing every trace of colour as her eyes flew to meet his.

'Bryony.' Rafe began to stride towards her, but she made an inarticulate sound and ran back upstairs, dropping the tray on to an antique chest on the landing, the delicate china cups bouncing on their saucers. But he was gaining on her and with a sob she flung open the door of Etta's room and ran in.

Etta was sitting at the dressing-table, touching up her lipstick after breakfast, and swung round in astonishment when Bryony burst in the room.

'Rafe's here,' she managed, just as he appeared in the doorway behind her.

She didn't look at him, couldn't, and went to gaze unseeingly out of the window as Etta got to her feet and said angrily, 'What on earth are you doing here?'

'I'm sorry.' Rafe's voice for once sounded unsteady. 'I thought there was something wrong with Bryony so I came after her.' His voice changed, became imperative. 'Is there something wrong, Bryony?'

But she didn't turn round, didn't give in to his unspoken command to look at him.

'Bryony's fine,' Etta said. 'Why are you here at the

house?' And she walked forward, gesturing him ahead
of her out of the room and closing the door behind her.

Bryony heard their voices receding down the stairs,
and only when the house was silent again realised how
loudly her heart was thumping, and that her hands were
still shaking. Running through the house to the old
tower, she climbed the steep stairs to the second floor
and a window overlooking the driveway and the chapel,
then watched Etta and Rafe standing together, talking
to a man who looked as if he was in charge of the
workmen. They were there longer than she expected;
she hadn't thought that Etta would be so interested in
seeing the men unload their equipment. Then she
realised that Etta wasn't going to risk leaving Rafe
alone. He must have realised it, too, because he gave
the house a long, lingering look, then briskly nodded to
Etta, climbed into his car and left.

Her shoulders slumping in relief, Bryony went down
to meet Etta.

'Thanks for trying to warn me,' the older woman
said. 'What a nerve he had chasing after you like that!
He probably thought he'd have a chance to look round
the house before I came down.'

'Does he suspect about the hotel, do you think?'
Bryony asked, grateful that Etta hadn't seen anything
in Rafe's visit beyond her own problems.

'It's impossible to tell with Rafe; he never gives
anything away.' Etta gave an angry shrug. 'Let's forget
him.'

But that was impossible for them both, though for
far different reasons. Bryony felt an ache deep within
her that wouldn't go away, a longing to be close to him,
not only for the fulfilment of desire, but just to be held
in his arms, to touch him and hear his voice — emotions
so deep and desperate that she could think of little else.
Every other emotion she had ever felt paled into

nothingness compared to this. She had thought herself
in love with Jeff and had looked forward eagerly to
being with him, but there had never been this ache of
need, this desolation because she knew she would never
be held in Rafe's arms again.

On Wednesday morning Bryony washed her hair,
drying it into a loose, swirling mane about her head,
then put on her new clothes. Her cheekbones were
more finely drawn now and her eyes seemed larger,
giving her a haunting look of loveliness. She looked
good, but she didn't care. She was only going to this
charity lunch because Etta had insisted on it.

Giovanni drove them in the Rolls, along the coast
road to the hotel that overlooked the sea. The foyer
was already crowded and Bryony was surprised to see
almost as many men as women there; she had expected
it to be an all-female affair. They helped themselves to
glasses of champagne from the waiting trays and began
to circulate, meeting again some of the women to whom
she'd been introduced at Etta's tea-party a few weeks
ago. Etta was enjoying herself, being addressed as
'Contessa', and swapping gossip with her friends, but
Bryony felt completely detached, although she came in
for quite a lot of attention herself. She was so much
taller than most of the women, although there were one
or two other blondes.

She was chatting with a group who could only speak
Italian, Etta having wandered off, when she became
aware of being watched. Looking up, she saw Rafe
standing a few feet away. Immediately he walked
towards her, his hands slipped into his pockets in a
casual manner, but with an intentness in his eyes that
told her there was no running away this time. She
stopped speaking, her gaze held by his, and knew that
if he touched her she was lost.

'Ah, the elusive Miss Ferrers,' he said softly, and reached out to take her hand.

Putting her free arm behind her, Bryony gave him a cool nod and turned to carry on her conversation. But the women with her weren't so apparently immune to Rafe. 'Conte!' They greeted him with smiles and drew him into their circle. Bryony quickly moved away, looking for Etta, wanting to latch on to her and cling like a limpet until she could leave the party, which she intended should be as soon as possible. She would have to fake another stomach cramp or something and —

She should have known that Rafe wouldn't let her get away. Coming up behind her as she looked wildly round for Etta, he took a steel-like grip of her arm and said, 'I want to talk to you.'

'Take your hand off me or I'll scream. I mean it!' she said fiercely, her eyes spitting fire.

Rafe's face hardened and if anything his grip tightened. 'That isn't what you said the last time we met,' he reminded her shortly.

Bryony's face flamed. 'That was a — mistake,' she said unsteadily.

Leaning towards her, so that only she could hear, he said softly, 'How could such a wonderful night be a mistake, Bryony? *Mia cara*. . .'

'Don't call me that. And if you don't let me go I shall throw this drink in your face. I'm quite sure you wouldn't like that; it would draw too much attention to you. After all,' she added with bitter anger, 'you've probably had half the women here on your damn loveboat!'

Rafe let go her arm but he glared down at her. 'Don't be so melodramatic, Bryony. Just because you found —'

He jerked his head aside just in time to avoid most of her drink as she flung it at him, but a good deal of it went over his suit. A look of stunned amazement came into his eyes to be replaced by one of distinct menace. But Bryony didn't hang around to find out what he would do or say. She had caught sight of Etta and made a bee-line for her just as the doors into the dining-room were opened and the guests began to file in.

'Etta, I have to talk to you,' she said urgently, echoing Rafe's words.

But Etta was listening deferentially to another woman and merely put out a hand to draw Bryony into the room beside her. Not given a chance to protest, she followed the women into a huge room set with round tables and decorated with a mass of beautiful flower arrangements. Having no choice, she sat down beside Etta and was relieved to have the seat next to her taken by a benign-looking man with a beard and middle-aged spread. He murmured his name but Bryony was so busy looking to see where Rafe was sitting that she didn't hear, just said her own name quickly in return. At first she couldn't see him, but then he came through the doors, after everyone else, and she realised he must have been trying to wipe off the champagne she'd thrown at him.

Bryony ducked her head down and began a vivacious conversation with her rather surprised neighbour, but she watched Rafe out of the corner of her eye as he made his way to a table only three rows down. She would have liked to know whom he was with, but it was impossible to see in the crowded room. The lunch was served, a series of dishes that Bryony was sure would have been delicious if she could have brought herself to eat anything. Instead she drank her wine and gave the man next to her all her attention, astounding him with her fluency in Italian and making him laugh at her dry, nervous wit.

'You seem to be enjoying yourself.' Etta turned to her with a smile. 'I'm glad I insisted that you came.'

Bryony groaned inside but smiled brilliantly back. 'Yes, I'm having a marvellous time, thank you. Did you notice that Rafe is here?'

'Really? He doesn't usually come to lunch parties, especially on working days. I wonder why he's here?'

'Perhaps there's someone here he wants to see, a girlfriend, maybe,' Bryony suggested, wondering if it was true. He certainly hadn't come here especially to see *her*, that was for sure, because he hadn't known she was coming.

'He isn't seeing anyone that I know of,' Etta remarked. 'And I'm sure I would have heard if he was.'

'I hadn't realised that he'd inherited the title as well as everything else from Antonio. I suppose that makes him rather eligible.'

Etta nodded. 'One of the most eligible men on the island, I should imagine.'

'Will he marry a Sicilian girl, do you think?'

'Who knows? He may meet someone in Rome.'

'But isn't he expected to marry a local girl, someone suitable?'

'Of course not. He's a man, he can marry whom he chooses — as long as she's from a good, preferably wealthy family, Italian, and a virgin,' Etta added wryly.

Bryony sat back in her chair. Well, that certainly lets me out, she thought bitterly. And I've been fool enough to let myself fall in love with the man.

There were a lot of speeches during the meal, the presentation of a cheque to the charity, and general congratulations all round to the people who had raised the money and to those who had donated it. Coffee was served and people began to drift from table to table, talking to their friends. Bryony began to get worried that Rafe would come over; that look in his eyes after she'd thrown the champagne at him had been distinctly dangerous, and she had the uncomfortable idea that he wasn't the kind of man who would just ignore something like that. But she saw him stand up and wait for a girl he was sitting with to get to her feet, a young girl, smart, short, and with the richly dark hair of a native Sicilian.

They moved over to another table further down the room and Bryony became aware that her neighbour was talking to her. During lunch he had been telling her about the gaily painted carts that had once been common on the island, but were seldom seen now that it had become a status symbol among Sicilians to own at least one car per family. He'd mentioned that there was an old cart in the hotel, a feature of one of the bars, and now he asked if she'd like to see it. With Rafe out of the way she was pleased to go and let him escort her back to the wide foyer of the hotel and into a quiet cocktail bar opening off it, empty now in mid-afternoon.

The cart, basically red, was richly carved, its panels painted with scenes depicting the Norman, Roger de Hauteville, and his men, who captured the island from the Saracens in the eleventh century. An ancestor of Rafe's? Bryony wondered, running her fingers over the carving. Her companion began to tell her about the puppet theatres on the island, which had plays based on the Norman conquest, but he broke off to smile and hold out his hand in greeting as Rafe came into the room, the girl she had seen him with earlier still at his side.

The two men shook hands, speaking to each other like old friends, although there was a deference to age and maturity in Rafe's voice. Bryony looked at the girl. She was very young, only about seventeen, and wore some good jewellery. Definitely rich. Definitely Italian.

Definitely a virgin. 'I think you've met my cousin, Paola Laneri,' Rafe was saying.

'Of course. Of course.'

Rafe turned to Bryony and introduced the two girls. 'Paola sometimes acts as crew on my boat,' he added, his voice expressive.

Their eyes clashed for a moment until Bryony looked away. So was she supposed to think that the bracelet had been the girl's, and that because she was his cousin she was innocent, and therefore he had never made love to any other woman on the yacht?

Before she could even begin to think about it, the girl said in uncertain English, 'Bryony? That is a pretty name. Please, what does it mean?'

'It's the name of a flower,' Bryony replied, then glanced at Rafe. 'A wild white flower that grows only in English hedgerows.'

'I think I've heard of it.' His voice was polite, merely social. 'It's a climbing plant, isn't it? One that clings to old branches.'

'I'm surprised you noticed,' Bryony answered, her verbal foil as sharp as his. 'After all, it's a very insignificant flower.'

A sudden light flashed in his eyes. 'Not when it transforms the hedge and makes it beautiful.'

Taken aback by his forcefulness, Bryony grew very still for a moment, but then turned quickly away to smile at the younger girl. 'Have you seen this cart? It's very interesting.'

Paola politely looked at the cart with her while the two men talked together. 'Please, may we speak in English?' the girl asked. 'I need to practise for my — my school test.'

'Your exams? You're still at school?'

'Yes. And I hope to go to university.'

So Rafe would have a long wait if it was this girl he

wanted to marry. 'Did Rafe — Raphael — say that you're
his cousin?'

'Yes, but not a — not a close cousin. His mother and
my mother, they were cousins.'

'Oh, I see. You mean you're second cousins.'

'Yes, that is it.' Paola gave her a delighted smile.
'See how you help me with my English. Do you stay
long in Sicily? I would like to talk with you again.'

Bryony murmured that she didn't know. She was
very aware of Rafe behind her, knowing that he was
watching. Her heart was thumping, and she was trying
to think of some way, short of just walking rudely away,
that she could get back to Etta and leave. It was her
lunch companion who solved the problem for her, but
the wrong way. Coming up to them, he said, 'Have you
said hello to my wife yet, Paola? No? Then you must
come with me to find her; she would be very sorry not
to see you again.' And, taking the younger girl's arm,
he firmly escorted her back to the dining-room.

Bryony went to follow them but Rafe moved to bar
the way. She gave him an angry glance. 'That was very
opportune.'

'No, I asked him to leave us alone for a few minutes,'
he admitted, confirming her suspicions. He stood
regarding her for a few seconds, then gave a twisted
smile. 'How angry you are, Bryony. I assure you that
was Paola's bracelet. You can ask her, if you like.
Believe me, you have nothing to be jealous of.'

'I am not — jealous,' she said stiffly.

'No?' He lifted a disbelieving eyebrow.

'No! I just feel *used*.' He frowned, went to say
something, but she went on quickly, 'Oh, don't think I
blame you. I blame myself. After all, I knew about
your reputation, knew you were a womaniser.'

Rafe's face hardened and he moved nearer to her.
'There have been women in my life, yes.'

'Yes. You're very — experienced.' Her throat tightened and she found it difficult to speak. 'You know how to make love to a woman. How to please her.'

The frowning look deepened as Rafe tried to understand. 'Yes, I hope so.'

She bit her lip. 'It was a very polished performance. Very smooth. Very — enlightening.'

'I don't understand you, Bryony. What are you trying to say?'

'No, I don't suppose you do.' Her chin came up. 'I made a big mistake. I thought. . . Never mind what I thought. I realised I was just another woman to add to your list. Another body to practise your skills on. You made me feel — as if I was on a production line. And I —'

Lunging forward, Rafe caught her wrist. 'No, Bryony, that isn't how you felt and you know it,' he gritted, his accent strong. 'You had never known such love before. Not from this Englishman you're running away from.' Suddenly he lifted her hand, shook it. 'This bracelet you're wearing; did your Englishman give you that?'

She stared, disconcerted.

'Yes, probably he did. Or some other boyfriend in your past. You took presents from him, but mine you sent back to me without a word. Why, Bryony? Why?'

Confused, she sought for words, trying to pull her hand free but not succeeding. 'Because — because I felt cheap.' Her voice strengthened. 'Because it was almost like a payment for services rendered.'

His eyes, dark and intent, held hers. 'There was nothing cheap about what we shared, Bryony. In your heart you know that.'

'There was nothing spontaneous either,' she burst out. 'It wasn't — ' She broke off in distress, turning her head away, trying to break free of his hold. 'I don't want to get involved with you!'

'But you are involved, Bryony.' Putting his hand on her other arm, he began to draw her slowly towards him, his dark, intent eyes holding hers. She tried to draw away, made some murmur of protest, but his steel-like hands drew her closer still. Bryony stared at him, her eyes wide and vulnerable, unable to resist. 'You will always be involved,' he said softly. 'Now, and tomorrow, and tomorrow.'

CHAPTER SEVEN

FATE, which had been playing hell with her all morning, suddenly took pity on her and saved Bryony from the humiliation of Rafe's kiss. There was the sound of voices outside, and he quickly let her go, stepping away from her as the door opened and several people came into the bar. Who they were, Bryony didn't look to see; she was out of there and back in the dining-room with undignified haste. Quite a few people had already left and it was easy to spot Etta among those remaining.

Going up to her, Bryony took her arm in a grip as firm as that which Rafe had used on her, said with a brittle smile, 'Excuse us,' to the people Etta had been talking to and almost frog-marched the poor woman to the door.

'Bryony! What on earth——?' Etta broke off as she saw the hunted look in her eyes.

'I'm afraid we have to leave.' They came out of the hotel and were met by the waiting Giovanni. 'Where's the car?'

'The car is parked down the road, Contessa. I bring it.'

'No, we'll walk to it with you,' Bryony told him, and kept her hold on Etta's arm to hurry her along.

The older woman didn't complain until they were in the car, then she sat down with some relief, panting from the exertion of walking so fast in her high heels. 'Just what was all the panic?' she demanded as they pulled away. 'You rushed out of there as if the devil was after you.'

'He was,' Bryony answered shortly, and unhappily

141

realised that she would have to give Etta some expla-
nation. 'It was Rafe. He—he. . .'

'He propositioned you,' Etta guessed. 'I'm not surprised. But what a time and place to choose.'

'Why aren't you surprised?'

'Because he wants to annoy me. And because you
intrigue him. I told you anyone who played hard to get
would arouse him.' Bryony turned her head away,
letting her hair hide her flushed cheeks, but Etta
mistook her reasons and patted her arm comfortingly.
'And because you're beautiful too, of course. You're a
challenge Rafe can't resist. But just keep holding out
on him, dear; he won't like that at all.'

Bryony bit her lip, wanting to tell Etta the truth, but
convinced that the older woman would immediately put
her on the first plane back to England, hotel or no
hotel. And, although going home seemed suddenly like
a very good idea, Bryony had no wish to go there in
such humiliating circumstances. 'I don't ever want to
see him again,' she said vehemently.

Surprised, Etta raised her well-groomed eyebrows.
'What on earth did he say to you?'

Realising she was on dangerous ground, Bryony said,
'It doesn't matter. Did you see that girl he was with?
Paola Laneri. He said she was his cousin.'

'Yes, she is. Her parents were there too. I don't
know them very well; they're related to Rafe on his
mother's side.'

'He introduced me to her.'

'He did? I should hardly have thought. . .' Etta
shrugged. 'Rafe's a law unto himself, of course.'

'Why do you say that?'

'Well, dear, it seems strange that Rafe should intro-
duce you to his schoolgirl cousin one moment and
then proposition you the next. It isn't in character.'

'Meaning that a woman he wants to make his mistress

shouldn't be allowed to mix with an innocent young member of his family, right?'

'Right.'

They looked at each other, both puzzled, then Bryony sat back in her seat and sighed. 'Let's forget about him. Did you enjoy the party?'

'Very much,' Etta said with enthusiasm, happy to discuss it. 'Did you see that woman I was talking to as we went into lunch? It was the local Princess, one of the most aristocratic people on the island. She organises all the big charity functions, including the Red Cross ball next month. I was never invited to that until Antonio and I were married. And I don't think I would have been then, except that Antonio made a very large donation and they couldn't very well not invite me along with him,' she said candidly. 'It was because I was his mistress first, you see. The people who run it aren't really stuffy in themselves, but it's supposed to be an honour to be invited, so I suppose they have to be careful.'

'Doesn't she usually talk to you?' Bryony asked, pleased not to have to talk about Rafe.

'Oh, yes, but this will be the first ball since Antonio died and I wondered whether they might drop me from the invitation list now. Especially with Rafe using his influence against me.'

'But she was OK? You're going to be invited?'

'Yes.' Etta smiled in satisfaction. 'And you made a hit with Don Frederico.'

'Who?'

'Don Frederico. The man you were sitting next to at lunch. He and his wife are great friends of the Princess.'

'I didn't catch his name,' Bryony admitted. 'He reminded me a bit of my grandfather.' Which made Etta burst into laughter.

There weren't any guests around that afternoon so

Bryony went down to the pool to sunbathe — and also to give serious thought to going home. Because today had proved that she was far from immune to Rafe. No matter how angry and humiliated she felt, there was no armour against this desperate need he aroused in her. She couldn't have stopped him kissing her today, she knew that. Knew that she had wanted him to with all her soul. I'm lost, she thought. I've fallen headlong for entirely the wrong man and there's nothing I can do about it. Except run away. Run back to England and hide.

The idea seemed both attractive and impossible. How can I go and never see him again? she thought with dismay. How can I live the rest of my life knowing that he's here, probably loving someone else, just as he loved me? Loving them, using them, leaving them, she thought bitterly. But oh, with what memories!

I must go, she decided in despair. I must get away from here as fast as I can, make sure I don't see him again. If I'm to avoid being really hurt, then I must find the courage — because it would take courage — to leave. It's the only way. Bryony sat up, ready to go and pack, but then she saw Etta sitting on one of the rattan chairs on the terrace, snoozing off her lunch in the sun, and was immediately filled with guilt. I can't just abandon her, run away like a thief in the night. Especially when the hotel seems to be going so well. Why, last night she was even talking about having the tower made into a suite of rooms. I've either got to stay or else find someone else to take my place.

Completely torn, Bryony decided that work was the only panacea, and went inside to change before going down to the kitchen to start vigorously making pastry, throwing it down on the marble slab as if she hated it. The result was some delicious hors-d'oeuvres cases that she filled and served at dinner that night, although John

Cornell was the only guest, one couple having left the day before, and the other guests, three ladies who were making an archaeological tour, having gone to Taormina for the evening. He and Etta seemed happy enough with each other's company, though, chatting away as if they were old friends, although Etta hadn't seemed to like him at first.

After serving dinner, Bryony ate alone, Giovanni having driven the ladies into Taormina and Maria taking the opportunity to visit a friend in the village, one of the women who came to help clean the villa. It was a very warm night. Bryony tried to concentrate on writing a letter to her parents but found it impossible. There was too much she couldn't tell them, although they would have understood. She toyed with the idea of phoning them, but knew that if she did her mother would immediately guess from her voice that something was wrong. It would mean either blurting everything out over the phone or else hedging, in which case her parents would probably be on the first plane over here to find out what was the matter. They still talked of coming to the villa as hotel guests, but her father, a research chemist, was involved in a series of experiments at the moment and couldn't get the time off. Bryony had been disappointed about that, but now was rather glad; doting, anxious parents would be too much to handle on top of everything else.

Too restless to read or watch television, Bryony wandered through the villa, checking that everything was tidy and in order. From behind the sitting-room door she could hear the sound of Etta's laugh; she must still be with John Cornell, who had decided to stay on for yet another week. Giovanni brought the three ladies home and Bryony made them a nightcap, but they were tired and soon went up to their rooms. Restless still, she went out of the house and into the garden, then,

drawn irresistibly, she took the path that led to the
beach. There was no one waiting at the jetty tonight.
No flag flew at the masthead. She wouldn't be held and
kissed and loved until she cried out with the sheer
ecstasy of it. In time she might meet someone else, she
supposed, might be made love to again. But it would
never be the same, never be so sensuous, never be so
skilful.

Again she came back to that. Bryony stood for a long
time gazing out to sea, then she turned and went back
inside.

She was the last to go up, making sure the front door
was bolted, the lights, except for one on the landing,
turned off. It was no use trying to read again; as soon
as she got into bed Bryony turned off the light, lay
awake for a while feeling thoroughly wretched, and
eventually fell asleep.

It was the most wonderful dream. Rafe was kissing
her, his lips light as a summer breeze on her skin. He
kissed her throat, the line of her jaw, merely touched
her lips before he moved on to her eyes. They were
little soft kisses that nevertheless excited her and made
her moan with longing in her sleep. She stirred, murmured his name, felt his hand caressing her, and sighed
with pleasure. His lips came back to her mouth, became
firm, insistent — and suddenly she was awake and he
was there. No dream. A living, breathing reality.
Bryony gave a gasp of fright, but he murmured soothingly, his hands caressing her bare shoulders.

'How did you get in here?' she demanded, too
stunned yet to be angry.

He chuckled, his head close to hers. 'I've lived in this
house nearly all my life; I'll always be able to find a
way in.'

Into the house and into her bed, she realised as she
moved and felt his long length against her own. He was

naked, too; she found that out when she put up a hand
and tried to move away from him. She gasped. 'You've
got a nerve! Get the hell——'

Leaning over, Rafe kissed her again, his hand holding
her head still as his shoulders hunched in growing
passion. She didn't protest again, not even when he
lifted the nightshirt over her head and began to caress
her all the way down, his lips following his hands, not
even when, succumbing to passion, he took her in a
blaze of hunger, lifting them both to a shared eruption
of excitement.

Afterwards, lying in his arms, knowing that she was
lost forever, Bryony said wryly, 'Was that to pay me
back for throwing the champagne in your face?'

He laughed, making her turn quickly towards him,
wishing that she could see his face in the darkness.
'That was because I've been going mad with wanting
you for nearly two weeks.'

'Well, now you've had me,' she said shortly.

'For the moment,' Rafe agreed. He kissed her neck.
'Why are you so angry with me, *cara*?' She didn't
answer at once and his voice hardened. 'Are you still in
love with your Englishman; is that it?'

She didn't attempt to deny that there *had* been an
Englishman. 'No.'

'But you did love him?' Rafe persisted.

'I thought I did,' she admitted. 'Yes, I really thought
I was in love with him, but I didn't know then.'

'Didn't know what?'

Avoiding the truth, she said, 'I didn't know how to
tell the difference between love and infatuation.'

'And you found out you weren't in love with him any
more.' He sounded pleased.

'Something like that.'

'But you came to Sicily to forget him?'

'Perhaps.'

'And now you have forgotten him.' It was a statement of certainty, not a question. 'Now that we are lovers you think only of me, yes?'

'You arrogant devil! What makes you think I care about you?'

Rafe chuckled richly. 'My darling Bryony, you are hardly in a position to deny it.'

That made her laugh — and suddenly she knew that she was happy. Supremely, exultantly happy. OK, so maybe the future held pain and humiliation at this man's hands, but right now she was in love and she was as close to him as she would ever be. There was no pride left. Not even fear. Only this overwhelming happiness. There would be no bright, shining future, but the present was a flame that could never burn so richly, be so all-consuming. So forget the future; she would live only for now, and would treasure this present happiness for the rest of her life. But perhaps it would be better not to let Rafe know that; better to play it cool.

So Bryony said, 'You're crazy coming here like this. What if someone should see or hear you?'

'Etta's room is on the other side of the house.'

'Yes, but there are — she has friends staying.'

'It seems that Etta has invited all her friends to stay lately. A whole procession of them,' Rafe said lightly. 'If any of them see me, they'll just think I'm another hotel guest — sorry, we're calling them friends, aren't we?'

Reaching out, Bryony turned on the bedside lamp so that she could see him. 'You know.'

'Of course I know. Did Etta really think she could keep something like that a secret?'

'She hoped to,' Bryony admitted. 'How did you find out?'

'I heard a rumour, then I talked to one of the guests and he confirmed it.'

'The American, when you were on the boat?' Rafe nodded. 'Etta was afraid he might have given the game away.' She gave him a contemplative look. 'She said that you would do all you could to oppose her, that you had the power to force her to close. Have you?'

'Yes.'

'And will you?'

He didn't answer directly, instead lifting a hand to stroke her hair as it lay on her bare shoulder, and said, 'You have beautiful hair, *cara*.'

'Thank you.'

Smiling at her formal politeness, he said. 'One day I am going to teach you the proper way to accept a compliment, especially one paid in circumstances like these.'

'Is there a special way, then?'

'Oh, definitely. You see, you have to ——'

She put a hand over his lips. 'Don't change the subject, Rafe. Are you going to close Etta down?'

He gave her a brooding look, then said, 'What is your part in this?'

There was no point now in trying to hide the truth. 'I work here. I do the cooking and help run the hotel.'

'Were you—recruited? Did Etta advertise to find you?'

She sensed a tension in his tone that the question didn't deserve, and gave him a puzzled look. 'She could hardly advertise if she wanted to keep the whole thing a secret. No, I've got a cordon bleu certificate and I was at a loose end so I accepted her offer of a job and came out here.'

'What do you mean "at a loose end"?'

'Literally it means I had nothing to do; I was uncertain about my future.'

'And particularly?'

'Particularly I suppose it means that Jeff and I had split up but I hadn't got round to looking for a job.'

'You lived with him?'

'We shared a place, yes.'

'But you didn't work when you were with him?'

'No.' She said it a little defiantly, knowing what he would think.

But he said, 'A man should take care of his mistress.'

'I wasn't. . . We didn't think of it the way you do. Lots of people live together permanently in Britain. They consider themselves to be partners. They just don't consider it necessary to get married to make a commitment to each other any more, that's all.'

'How convenient, especially if the man tires and walks away, as your boyfriend did,' he said sardonically.

'He didn't tire of me!' she exclaimed hotly. 'It was a mutual agreement.'

'Were you happy with him?'

'Yes, very, for the first year or so.'

'How long were you with him?'

'Actually living with him for about eighteen months, but I knew him for a few months before that.' This last a sop to her own pride, to let him know that she didn't just fall into bed with a man. 'Then we started to drift apart.'

'But you came here to get over it,' Rafe pointed out.

She gave him a taunting smile. 'No, as a matter of fact I came here simply because I thought I would enjoy the challenge. We deliberately let the rumour that I was recovering from a broken heart circulate, knowing you would hear. Etta thought it would account for my being here while we got the hotel ready, and also make you leave me alone.'

'Did she, indeed?' Rafe sat up and leaned against the

pillows as he grinned down at her. 'How very cunning. Well, it worked for the first part but not for the second. It definitely didn't keep me away from you.'

Rolling on to her stomach, Bryony propped herself on her elbows, her chin on her fists. 'No. If anything I think it intrigued you, made you want to take advantage of my vulnerability.'

'But you say you were not broken-hearted.'

'No, but you weren't to know that. You could have been out to get me on the rebound.'

He frowned a little. 'Do you really think that?'

'How do you know I'm not on the rebound?' she countered.

Leaning down, he kissed the end of her nose and then her mouth. 'I wanted you before I heard about your broken romance. You know that. And I don't think, *mia cara*, that you have ever been completely immune to me.' His kiss deepened and he reached to fondle her. Bryony surrendered to it, the flame kindling deep within her, making her reach eagerly for his lips. His voice husky, Rafe said, 'I think the time has come to give you that lesson.'

She leaned away from him, her eyes mischievous. 'Well, if you ever paid me any decent compliments, you might be surprised at how I'd react.'

His eyes glinted with amused concupiscence. 'That is a definite challenge. So, my darling, if I tell you that the thought of you keeps me awake all night, that I ache to be near you like this, and yet nearer?'

'Not bad,' Bryony murmured a little breathlessly. 'But you'll have to do much better.'

Rafe drew her towards him, his eyes hungry now and his voice urgent. 'And if I told you that the sight of your beauty sets my heart on fire, that your loveliness is beyond compare? And I want you, need you, long for you?'

'Well, then.' She moved over him, her voice hoarse
with anticipation. 'Then I'd react like this. And—and
like this.'

He gasped, stood it for several minutes, then pulled
her down so that he could kiss and make love to her
with a depth of passion he hadn't before shown.

Bryony was asleep when he left her bed, but some
movement roused her a little and she reached out for
him. 'Rafe?'

He leaned over the bed to kiss her. 'Go back to
sleep, *cara*.' And he stroked her hair until her eyes
closed again.

But the clicking of the door-latch and its soft closure
roused her again, making her blink heavy-lidded eyes
in the darkness. No, not complete darkness; the faint
greyness of morning was stealing between the curtains.
Bryony smiled to herself, remembering Rafe's pleased
surprise at her response to his lovemaking. That first
time she had taken; last night she had given in return.
She snuggled into the covers like a contented cat, would
have purred if she'd been one. Life was very, very
wonderful again. Idly, still half asleep, she wondered
how he would get out of the house; the same way as
he'd got in, presumably, although he hadn't told her
how. Bryony chuckled a little, wondering what Rafe
would do if he ran into one of the guests, especially one
of the three spinster ladies. If she'd any sense, Bryony
thought with a giggle, she'd grab him and pull him into
her room.

Smiling to herself, she lay in the bed still warm from
his body, going back over the night, fixing it in her
memory. But then she recalled their conversation
earlier and a slight, uneasy chill filled her. Rafe had
given her no assurances about the hotel, had cleverly
avoided giving her a straight answer more than once.
What would he do about it? she wondered. And if it

came to that, what would he do about her? He hadn't said when he would see her again, or even if he wanted to. But he must be very sure of her now, know that he had only to fly the flag at the masthead for her to run to the boat, or to make a phone call that would take her to a hotel or his flat to meet him.

'A man should take care of his mistress.' Rafe's words echoed in her brain. He'd said it almost approvingly, although he'd asked too many questions about Jeff not to give away a basic jealousy. Deciding, with more than a little chagrin at her own lack of resistance where Rafe was concerned, that she could now be classed as a mistress rather than a one-night stand, Bryony wondered just how Rafe intended to take care of her. Perhaps he might want her to leave the villa and move in with him — which would be letting poor Etta down even more than if she went home. It would be a betrayal, a going over to the enemy. So that was out, because she felt that falling in love with Rafe was betrayal enough already.

So what, then? Would he be content with the occasional snatched hour on the boat, or the risk of a scandal if he continued to sneak into the villa? Somehow Bryony couldn't imagine his pride allowing that for long. And would he want to take her out, meet his friends or even his family? Bryony couldn't imagine that happening either, which saddened her. Although he had introduced her to his young cousin. But that surely had been part of his ploy to get her alone at the charity lunch; he'd needed the cousin as an excuse to get rid of Don Frederico.

Having lived in Milan for several months, Bryony knew something of Italian moral standards, but she strongly suspected from what Etta had said that here in Sicily they were far more rigid. She had been brought up to have a high regard for herself, as a person, and for her own body. She had never had occasional affairs, respecting herself too much to give the gift of her body, in which she took a proper pride, to a casual lover. Jeff had been the first man in her life, and up until Rafe the only one. Knowing this, she still had her own pride, but now she felt that she was lower in Rafe's estimation and, if it became known, probably in that of Sicilian society. And that hurt. She didn't want to be treated like a kept woman, someone to be taken to places where Rafe wouldn't run any risk of meeting his family, to be brought out and rubbed down only for occasions where it wouldn't matter.

Bryony wasn't ashamed of loving Rafe—how could anyone ever be ashamed of love, for heaven's sake? It wasn't something you asked to happen, you couldn't decide 'I will love this man but I won't love that one'. It was fate that decided, that played cat and mouse, that made two people who were complete opposites end up with one another, or made her fall for a man who would never love her in return. Trying to look at the situation realistically, Bryony decided that Rafe was as close now as he would ever be to caring about her, so she'd just better make the most of it. There was no point in wasting this time by miserably hoping for more. She would take of Rafe what he cared to give, even if it was only his body, and try to be content with that. A humble decision that was alien to her nature, but she might never know love like this again, and she was determined to make the most of what she had.

The light was much brighter now and she didn't want to sleep. Putting on her swimsuit, Bryony ran down to the beach, along the jetty, and dived into the sea, swimming vigorously for about twenty minutes, then treading water to watch the sun lose its last grip on the horizon and begin its climb up the sky, golden and shimmering in the haze of morning. She stared in awe, aware suddenly of how small and trivial she was in the scheme of time and space. But I'll remember this moment always, she vowed, and when I feel low or desperate then I'll look back on this morning and remember how happy it's possible to be, and how beautiful the dawn.

This morning their three lady guests wanted to go to Palermo and Bryony was to act as translator rather than guide as she had never been there before. They hired a car to take them, but it was just an ordinary car they'd hired for the whole holiday, and one of the women intended to drive, which she did with dogged determination. It was a long way but they got there eventually, although there had been several nerve-racking occasions when the brakes had been slammed on and Bryony had begun to doubt that they would ever make it.

Keen amateur archaeologists, they went first to the seventeenth-century monastery that housed the museum of priceless artefacts found in the many ancient sites on the island. Leaving there after a couple of hours, they then walked through the lively, noisy streets to pay only a cursory visit to the cathedral before exploring the Corso Vittorio Emanuele with its many beautiful *palazzi*, churches and fountains. Palermo had a different air about it from Catania. It even smelt different when you got away from the exhaust fumes. The air was redolent of the spices that had been brought to the ancient port for over two thousand years, from the East and from Africa, carried on oar-driven biremes and ancient sailing boats, giving Palermo its life and prosperity.

Bryony could have lingered in the town, but the three ladies, after a light lunch in a pavement café at a table shaded partly by a palm tree that leaned over a garden wall and partly by lines of washing hung across the

narrow back street, wanted to move on. All very
practical women, they had worked out their schedule
beforehand, although they hadn't left enough time to
negotiate all the traffic they had met coming into the
town. So they were in a hurry to go on to the church of
St John of the Hermits, a strange but haunting mixture
of Arab and Norman architecture with small pink
cupolas like minarets against the clear blue of the sky.
But there were shady cloisters and a garden rich with
flowering shrubs where Bryony could sit alone for a
while and think of Rafe, and hope that he in turn was
thinking of her.

'You're daydreaming,' one of the women scolded.
But then her voice softened. 'It looked as if it was a
good dream.'

'Yes,' Bryony smiled, 'it was a good dream.'

The afternoon was very hot. They went back to the
car and drove out of the heat of the town up into the
coolness of the nearby mountains to Monte Pellegrino.
As the road climbed they could see far below them the
harbour at Palermo, and the off-shore islands that lay
like jewels in the sea, and, far off inland, the tip of
Mount Etna rising white-peaked against the distant sky.

'There's the sign.' One of the women pointed as they
neared the top of the mountain. ' "Santuario de Santa
Rosalia",' she read in an accent so terrible that they all
laughed.

There had been so much about Palermo to read up
that Bryony had missed this and didn't know what to
expect, but a guide took them into a cave in the rock
converted into a chapel, and Bryony, in her present
dreamlike mood, was immediately impressed with the
sanctity of the place, not so much by the statue and
painting of the saint's crowning, but by the simplicity of
the rock walls and the quietness. 'The walls are wet,'
she commented, putting out her fingers to touch.

'Mmm, the water is supposed to have miraculous properties.' The women came over to join her. 'I wonder if it can cure my rheumatism?' And one of them rubbed some over her elbow.

The others laughed and began to rub themselves in various places, then went to look around. But Bryony stayed where she was and let the water run over her hand, wishing, Let him love me, and yet afraid to wish for something so selfish in such a holy place.

They went for a walk along the mountain, then back to the car to drive to Addaura, where the women wanted to see the famous Paleolithic cave drawings, but were disappointed to find the caves closed and only able to be viewed by those getting special permission from the superintendent of ancient monuments at Palermo.

'We must come back tomorrow,' one of the women declared as they got back into the car.

'Why don't we stay in Palermo overnight?' another suggested, to Bryony's alarm.

She was eager now to get back, to see if Rafe had phoned, to see if there was a flag flying at the masthead. 'I have to cook dinner,' she said quickly.

So they took the *autostrada* across the centre of the island, all content with their day, and arrived back at the villa just as the heat went out of the long afternoon.

Maria had already started to prepare dinner, but gave a shake of her head to Bryony's eager enquiry about phone calls for her. 'You're sure? Perhaps the Contessa might have taken one for me.'

'No. I have been here all day. There were two calls for the Contessa from her friends, but nothing for you.' She gave Bryony a curious look. 'Do you expect a call?'

Managing a casual shrug, Bryony said, 'I thought my father might phone to say he'd received the parcel I sent for his birthday.' Quickly she changed the subject,

asking about the vegetables Maria was cutting, made
sure that everything was going well, then said, 'I'll just
run upstairs and change.'

She really did run, but to look out of the window at
the sailing-boat. There was no sign from Rafe, of
course—she hadn't really expected there to be; it was
much too early. Even so, she gave a small sigh of
disappointment, impatient to hear from him and be
with him again. The evening seemed to drag although
it was no different from any other. Tonight Etta asked
her to have dinner with her and the guests, a thing she
often did when the serving could be safely left to Maria
and Giovanni. Poor Mr Cornell, the only male, was
rather overwhelmed by numbers, although he didn't
seem to mind, sitting next to Etta and chatting away.
He had seemed rather an austere, almost argumentative
man when he had arrived in Sicily, but being on holiday
had made him relax dramatically. Originally he had
booked for only two weeks but seemed to have no
difficulty in extending his holiday, although he made
and received a great many calls and faxes to and from
New York. His phone bill was enormous, but he had
already paid most of it without turning a hair.

Tonight Bryony was impatient during her chat with
Etta, partly through guilt because she couldn't tell her
that Rafe knew about the hotel. But Etta was in no
mood to prolong their chat either, so it wasn't long
before Bryony could run up to her room to shower and
wash her hair, certain that Rafe would come. He did,
but earlier than she expected, arriving at the jetty in
the motorboat when it was still light. Hearing it, Bryony
went to the window, saw Rafe make the boat fast, but
instead of going on to the yacht as she expected he
walked deliberately up the beach towards the house.
Quickly pulling on white jeans, a shirt that knotted in
the front, leaving her waist bare, and a pair of trainers,

she ran downstairs in sudden fear, afraid that Rafe might be confronting Etta about the hotel right this minute.

He was in the hallway and facing Etta, but there were no accusations being thrown. Instead Rafe was standing in a ray of golden evening light from the open front door, hands casually in his pockets, asking about the chapel roof, whether Etta was satisfied with the work.

'Why, yes, they appear to have done a good job, thank you,' the older woman replied, a cautious note in her voice.

'I notice that the jetty is broken in a couple of places; perhaps I could have that repaired for you,' Rafe offered. Adding, as Etta's eyes widened in surprise, 'As I'm using it.'

'Oh, of course. Thank you.'

They both glanced up as Bryony came down the stairs and her heart gave a chest-beating thump at the sudden flare that came into Rafe's eyes when he saw her. 'Oh, hi, Rafe,' she managed with as much offhand nonchalance as she could.

His lips twitched. 'Hello, Bryony.' He turned to say goodbye to Etta. 'I thought I'd take the yacht out for a sail as it's such a warm evening.' He nodded to them both and started to leave, then stopped as if he'd just thought of something. 'Perhaps Bryony would like to come with me.'

'For a sail?' She pretended indifference and doubt, enjoying the game. 'Well, I don't know. I haven't done much sailing.'

'I would do all the work,' he offered, his eyes full of meaning. 'You could just be a passenger—unless you enjoyed it and wanted to try, of course,' he added.

She pretended to consider it further, then shrugged. 'Why not? But just once round the bay.' Turning politely to Etta, trying to hide the excited anticipation in her eyes, she said, 'Would you like to come with us?'

'I'm a little too old for that kind of thing. But thank you for the offer.' She gave Bryony a frowning look and put a hand on her arm. 'I think you'll need a sweater.'

'I'll get one.'

Bryony ran upstairs and when she came down found that Rafe had gone ahead of her to the boat. He was grinning to himself but wouldn't tell her what about until they had set sail and were heading out to sea. 'Etta warned me to behave myself,' he told her. 'She reminded me that you were under her care and that I was to leave you alone.'

'And do you intend to do as she says?'

'I'm afraid not,' he replied, grinning and putting an arm round her waist.

'Thank goodness for that! Otherwise I would have had to seduce you.'

'What an interesting idea.' Pulling her to him, he kissed her lingeringly. 'We must try it some time.'

'OK.' Her voice was husky as she clung to him, looking up into his eyes, her lips parted from the intensity of his kiss.

He laughed, a laugh of masculine possession and power. But then his eyes became a little guarded as he said, 'I must disobey Etta, then?'

'Yes, please.'

'Do her wishes for your welfare mean so little to you?'

Bryony frowned, not understanding where he was heading. 'I'm over eighteen. I've been of age for quite some time. Etta may feel responsible but I'm old enough to make my own decisions.'

'Ah, sì. As you did when you gave yourself to your Englishman.'

'Yes,' Bryony agreed, not knowing what to make of the flare of jealousy in his eyes. 'To him — *and only him.*'

Her stress on the words made him look at her tensely for a long moment. He seemed about to question her further but then changed his mind. 'How would you like to see Stromboli?' he asked her, deliberately changing the subject and his mood.

'The volcano? Great. When shall we go?'

'Now. We sail there. It's not only a volcano but an island.'

'But it will be dark by the time we get there, won't it?'

'That's the whole idea. The volcano is still active and the best time to see it is at night.'

'How long will it take?'

Rafe shrugged. 'Does it matter?'

She laughed suddenly and hugged him. 'Of course it doesn't. Let's go.'

They travelled north at a fast rate. They went parallel to the coast then through the narrow strait between Sicily and mainland Italy before hitting the open sea and bearing slightly west. It grew dark and they saw the lights of other islands, but then Rafe pointed ahead and she became aware of a deep red glow in the distant sky.

'Stromboli,' he said. 'The lighthouse of the Mediterranean.'

As they gradually drew nearer the fiery glow intensified and Bryony stared in fascination as the haze of colour focused into a river of molten lava rolling down a channel into the sea.

'They call that the *Sciara del Fuoco*,' he told her, turning off the engines.

The pit of fire. Bryony shivered and moved nearer to him, then gave a gasp of fright as an internal explosion sent a great plume of fiery, molten lava bursting into the air. 'Is it going to erupt?'

'No.' He put a reassuring hand on her shoulder. 'It does that all the time, although it is quite active tonight. A spectacle especially for you.'

'It's—awe-inspiring.' She gazed in wonder. 'Do people live on the island?'

'Yes, although nearly everyone has emigrated to America. They shut up their houses and vow to come back when they're rich.'

'If the houses are still there.'

'Yes.' He pointed again as an extra-thick wave of lava rolled down the mountainside. 'You see where the lava goes into the sea? It makes the water steam and boil. Even this far out the water is said to be warm.' He turned her to face him. 'Would you like to try it?'

'Go for a swim? Is it safe?'

'Yes, if we anchor the boat and keep near it.'

'I didn't bring a swimsuit with me.'

'Good.' He kissed her lightly. 'I hoped you hadn't.'

The water was warm, and it was one of the most beautiful experiences of Bryony's life. There was only a crescent moon but it was possible to see each other quite clearly by the red light from the lava flow. They were both good swimmers and Rafe chased her round the boat, caught and kissed her, before she slid away from his eager hands, laughing, teasing him to catch her again. But the third time he wouldn't let her go and held her against him, letting her know how much he wanted her, then hoisted her on board and swung himself up beside her. She turned to go into the cabin but he grabbed her arm and pulled her roughly to him, arching her under him as he kissed her fiercely.

If Bryony had wanted spontaneity then she had it now. With an incoherent sound he lowered her to their piled clothes on the deck, then came down on her with a compulsive urgency that left no time for the art or skill of lovemaking. He wanted her, needed her, *now*. For a moment, just before he climaxed, he raised himself up, mouth open in a shuddering moan, his eyes dark with passion, the flickering light of the molten lava playing on his long, muscular body. Then he said her name, not once, but over and over again, so that it echoed across the sea, then rose into a great cry of triumphant sexuality.

They made love just the once that night, both knowing that they had attained the very height of lovemaking. Dazed by it, and certainly exhausted, they dried themselves and dressed without speaking, then set off for home. Rafe sat at the tiller with her beside him, his arm round her. He was withdrawn, deep in his own thoughts, but there was nothing cold or reserved about it, because from time to time his arm tightened around her or he would kiss her hair. Bryony was content to sit there in silence, not thinking about anything very much, just completely happy, knowing that her place was with him and always would be.

It was only as the towns of Sicily slid past that she sensed a tension in him, a tension that grew as they passed Catania and he steered into the bay below the villa. Moving away from her, Rafe cut the speed of the engine so that they came quietly in. He moored quickly and efficiently, then came to help her off the boat and walk along the jetty with her, still silent, still very tense. Unable to bear the thought of any unease between them, Bryony stopped and looked at him. 'What is it, Rafe?'

He hesitated, then said, as if it was dragged from him, 'I have to know. I went to England to try and find out but couldn't.' He gripped her shoulders, so hard that he hurt her. 'Bryony, are you Etta's daughter? Are you?'

CHAPTER EIGHT

'Am I Etta's *daughter*?' Bryony gave a laugh of pure astonishment. 'Of course not! What on earth gave you that idea?'

Rafe's shoulders dropped as the tension left them and his grip eased in relief. 'I could think of no other reason for her giving you a home.'

'She didn't give me a home — she offered me a job.' There had been puzzlement in her voice, but now her face hardened as Bryony stepped away from him. 'Would it have mattered so much if I had been her daughter?'

He tried to shrug it off. 'I just wanted to know, that's all.' He went to put his arm round her waist again but she backed away.

'But it seems that it mattered so much to you that you went to England to try to find out.'

Rafe nodded reluctantly, as if he was sorry that he'd let it out. 'I thought that if she had an heir I'd have difficulty in getting the villa back, that's all.'

But Bryony was far ahead of him. 'And I suppose it might just have occurred to you that if you could prove that Etta had an illegitimate daughter you could tell the whole of Sicily about it, then she might be shamed into leaving. And then you'd have your precious villa back almost immediately, wouldn't you?' Her voice rose in anger and humiliation. 'And that's why you kept seeking me out when I first got here, because you were trying to find out who I was.'

'It wasn't the only reason,' he said swiftly, not trying

to deny it. 'I was—fascinated by you, even then. I wanted to know you better. Please believe me, Bryony.'

He put his arm out towards her but she turned and ran down the steps on to the sand so that he could hardly see her. Her laugh of bitterness came out of the darkness. 'Believe you? Why the hell should I? I always thought that there was something behind—behind all this. Etta said that you never did anything without a reason. Now I know what it is.'

'I admit that I thought she'd brought you here because it was safe to do so now that Antonio was dead. And at first. . .'

'Well? Go on, say it. You couldn't make me feel more humiliated than I do already,' she yelled at him.

'All right.' Angry himself now, Rafe jumped down the steps and strode up to her, his dark bulk looming out of the night. 'I thought that you were her daughter. You are not unlike her to look at and you said you were connected to her. And at first I thought that you would be like her in other ways.'

'What exactly do you mean by that?' she demanded furiously, knowing it would be yet another insult.

'Etta has had lovers all her life,' Rafe said baldly. Then made a throw-away gesture. 'Oh, I don't mean that she was a prostitute; there was never anything as sordid as that, as she insisted on only moving on to a new relationship when she was sure that it was going to be a semi-permanent one.'

'And you thought—you thought that I. . .' Bryony was so angry she couldn't get the words out.

'Yes, I admit I thought that. And I even wondered about her motives in bringing you here.' He paused, then added deliberately, 'Whether she intended you to entrap me.'

'Entrap you!' Bryony gave a gasp of rage, too angry to wonder what his choice of the word might mean. 'I'll have you know that I come from a very respectable family. I met Etta at my cousin's wedding. Etta went to school with her mother and is my cousin's godmother. *That's* how we're related, if you can call it that!' She swung away from him but then turned back. 'Etta offered me this job and I accepted because I thought it would be a challenge, would be fun. I didn't know that I was going to meet an arrogant swine who'd think it a good idea to seduce me just to find out what my character was like! Well, now you know, so make of it what you like. And—and to hell with you!'

This time she strode away, her dignity buoyed by rage, too furious yet to feel anguish.

'And I didn't know that I was going to fall in love with you,' Rafe shouted after her.

That brought her up short. She swung round, and cannoned into Rafe as he came after her. 'Damn it, I wish I could see!' Bryony exclaimed.

'Come back to the boat; we'll turn on the light. We'll talk this through.'

'No!' Putting out her hands, she pushed him away. 'I don't believe you. I'll never believe another word you say, *ever*. Come to that, I don't ever want to see you again.'

'Not even if I go down on my knees and swear it's the truth?'

'*You*? You wouldn't. You couldn't go down on your knees for any woman. I. . .' She heard him move and reached out, groping for him but not finding him. Then, in utter disbelief, Bryony lowered her hands and felt his head, level with her chest. 'But you——'

'For you I would.' He put his hands on her waist and resisted when she tried half-heartedly to push them off. 'Don't you understand, *cara*? You were the last girl in the world I wanted to fall for. I thought you were a danger to me, a seductress sent to entice me. So I decided to test you, but you slapped my face. And then I couldn't keep away from you, no matter how I tried, because I still wasn't sure. I went to England to try to find out who you were by going back into Etta's past, but I could find no trace of her having a child. But she could have kept it secret, perhaps had the child adopted. Waited until she was a respectable widow before she claimed you and brought you here. I just didn't know. Can you understand?'

He drew her down so that she knelt on the ground beside him, lowered his voice as he went on urgently, 'Everything about you told me that you weren't the same kind of woman as her, but then you admitted that you'd lived with a man.' His hands tightened. 'I was angry then and tried to forget about you. But I couldn't keep away. I *had* to see you again. I had to make love to you even though I thought I might be playing into Etta's hands. And after that night I knew I had to go on. I can't keep away from you. I'm bewitched by you, Bryony, *cara mia*. And every time we make love I become more crazy for you.' He paused, took a deep breath as if he was exhausted. 'Now do you understand?'

For a long moment she didn't answer, then Bryony pushed his arms aside and got to her feet. Lifting her head, she saw that the dawn was just beginning to break, the sky lightening on the horizon. 'Yes, I think I understand,' she said tonelessly. 'You were prepared to think the worst of me from the first moment we met, but you fell for me in spite of yourself. And that's still how you feel. How very flattering! Well, I'll make it easy for you. Just get out of my life and stay out! I never want to see you again.'

'That isn't true.' He came to his feet and put his arms round her. 'You know it isn't true.'

'No, it isn't.' She raised a strained face towards him.

'But right now I don't know how I feel about you. Just leave me alone, Rafe. Please. I have to—I have to think about this.' Breaking free from his hold, she ran up to the house. He followed, but didn't try to stop her. At the door she glanced back and saw his figure dark against the growing light. He made a gesture towards her with his hand, but she went inside and bolted the door.

It was darker inside the house; she had to wait a few moments for her eyes to adjust again, then went down the passage, through the kitchen and out into the hall. The light they left on all night on the upper landing lit the stairs for her. Etta was standing at the top of the flight, a deep blue robe over her nightdress. Slowly she came down the stairs to meet Bryony and gestured for her to go into the office, closing the door behind them.

'I've been very worried about you,' Etta said shortly. 'I was afraid you'd had an accident and been drowned.'

'I'm sorry. We—we went to Stromboli.'

'I see.' Etta gave her a searching look. 'Bryony, I have to ask this: are you and Rafe lovers?'

Bryony gave a high, unnatural laugh. 'I really don't know.'

'Don't know! My dear Bryony, that's hardly something you're not certain about.'

'No. Well, two hours ago I would have said yes. But then we got back here and Rafe—Rafe asked me whether I was your daughter.'

'He did *what*?'

'Not so surprising, really. He had the idea that I'd been brought out here to seduce him, so that he'd relent and let you go on living here in peace.' Lifting her head, Bryony gave Etta a straight look. '*Is* that why you offered me this job, Etta? Was that in your mind the whole time?'

'Of course not!' Etta exclaimed in indignation.

'No? After all, you did say it wouldn't be a bad idea for me to go out with Rafe, to get close to him so that he'd confide in me. That was exactly what you said. Oh, OK, you glossed over it, but you helped this along all you could, sending me out in the Rolls, telling Rafe where he could find me. And I bet you knew he'd be at that charity lunch.'

The older woman looked at her angry face then turned away with a shrug. 'I admit that I wasn't averse to you falling for each other, but I swear it hadn't even occurred to me when I asked you to join me. It was only when Rafe started to show an interest that I decided to encourage things a little. And what was wrong with that?' she added spiritedly. 'I hoped that a little romance might make him more human.'

'You mean more amenable about the villa, don't you?'

Etta smiled slightly. 'Yes, of course I do.'

'You're pretty good at manipulating people, aren't you? I suppose it comes from handling all those lovers you've had.'

Looking pained, Etta said, 'Rafe threw that at me, did he? Hardly a gentlemanly thing to do. And not very kind of you either, Bryony. After all I did bring you out here and——'

'And I have worked darn hard to get this place going, so don't try moral blackmail. I don't owe you any favours, Etta.'

The older woman looked as if she didn't agree, but said, 'What are you going to do now?'

'Right now I'm going to bed. And tomorrow you'll have to run the place and see to the cooking yourself, because I'm going to take the day off. I need to think things through in peace.'

She left Etta in the office but when she got to her room it was almost fully light and she couldn't sleep, even though she drew the curtains to shut out the morning. After a couple of hours she gave up trying, went down to the pool to swim, then put on a fresh swimsuit under shorts and a shirt and ran down to the village to catch the local bus, sitting next to the window to look at fields drowned in almond blossom as it rattled to the bus station in Catania. There she caught another bus to Mazzaró, the beach below Taormina, walked along to a less crowded spot and lay down on a towel to sunbathe. Sunbathe and think. Lost and ignored in the mass of tourists, able to go over everything in her mind at her leisure.

Bryony stayed on the beach the whole day, sometimes sunbathing, sometimes falling asleep in the shade of a hired beach umbrella, her sunglasses shading her eyes, hiding the fact that her thoughts were miles away. Only when the sun went down did she pick up her towel and walk to a café where she bought herself a meal, taking her time over it, so that it was almost ten o'clock before she got back to the villa.

Dinner was long over and she could see the guests through the drawing-room window, Etta sitting next to John Cornell on the settee, the three ladies at a table — working out the next day's schedule, probably. And standing by the fireplace, his fingers drumming impatiently on the mantelshelf, was Rafe. Bryony stood looking in for a minute or so, then went round the house to go in by the side-door. She said hello to Maria and Giovanni, and went up the back stairs to her room. She switched on the light, then stood in open-mouthed wonder. Her room was full of flowers, so many that the vases and arrangements filled every shelf and window-sill, and even stood on the floor.

Her first thought was that Rafe must have bought up the whole stock of a florist's shop, because that was what the room looked like. She frowned, thinking it overdone. Just one bouquet would have conveyed the message he wanted to get to her, or even one flower, like the single, perfect cream rose that lay in its box on her bed. The card with it bore only the initial 'R'. Taking out the flower, she held it to her lips, then reluctantly looked at all the other flowers, thinking that it wasn't like Rafe to overdo things. His taste was always understated, not flashy, like these exotic bird of paradise flowers and large, brightly coloured lily and aster-like blooms.

Bryony showered and put on a full-skirted blue dress in a soft, floating material, then hesitated for a moment before picking up a couple of baskets of flowers and carrying them downstairs. The drawing-room door was open and Etta on the watch for her, because she came out into the hall as soon as she saw Bryony come down.

Closing the door behind her, Etta said, 'Maria told me you were back. Rafe is here.'

'Yes, I saw him through the window.' She lifted one of the baskets of flowers. 'He rather overdid——'

But Etta interrupted her, saying urgently, 'There have been several phone calls for you. It seems that——'

She broke off as the door behind her opened and Rafe came out to join them. 'Bryony?' His eyes went to her face, eager, searching.

'Hello, Rafe.' She gave him an uncertain smile and laughed as she nodded at the basket she was holding. 'Thanks for the flowers. I'm overwhelmed by them all.'

'All?' His eyebrows rose as he looked at the baskets. 'But I only sent. . . It seems you have another—admirer,' he said drily.

'They're not from you? But I don't understand.'

'I haven't had a chance to tell you,' Etta said reluctantly. 'If I could just speak to you in private for a moment.'

'No, why don't you say it here?' Rafe insisted, his voice suddenly soft and menacing.

'I really don't——'

'You said there were some phone calls for me,' Bryony broke in. 'Who from—my parents? Surely they haven't sent me all these flowers?'

'No.' Etta hesitated, then shrugged. 'The calls were from someone called Jeff. He said you would know who he is.'

'Jeff?' Bryony's face paled a little.

'Yes. He was the one who sent all the flowers. Except for the one rose from Rafe.' And Etta sent him a half-reproachful, half-resentful look. 'Jeff said to tell you that he's in Rome and will fly here tomorrow. He also said——' Etta gave Rafe another glance, then lifted her chin defiantly '—that he's still in love with you and wants to marry you.'

Bryony's mouth dropped open in astonishment, but she turned quickly to Rafe as he began to laugh harshly. 'Do you really think I'm as gullible as my uncle was, Etta?' Then he turned to Bryony with something like a snarl. 'Or was this your idea? Were you afraid I wouldn't marry you, was that it? So you cooked up this idea to make me jealous, to make me think that I might lose you?' He laughed again, the sound raw and strident in the echoing hall. 'Then let me tell you that I was so crazy about you that I was already willing to give up all my principles, my freedom, the commitment to my family—everything. I came here tonight expressly to ask you to marry me. You see, you had no need of this—this trick you have played.'

'But I haven't!'

'It's no trick.'

Bryony and Etta spoke together, but Rafe said fiercely, 'Etta used this ploy to get my uncle to marry her. I had the man she'd been living with traced in

Australia. He never sent her any letter; he was living happily with his wife. But by the time I found out it was too late and my uncle had married her. And that's why I want her out of this house, out of the family she tricked her way into.' Going up to Bryony, he grabbed her arms violently, making her drop the baskets of flowers. 'I ought to thank you! I've been a fool, a lovesick fool. But you've opened my eyes in time. You've saved me from letting a second woman trick her way into this house!'

Letting her go, he strode towards the door, then turned as he reached it. 'I'll have this — hotel closed within a week. And find a way to have you thrown out just as soon as I can!'

The door slammed shut after him, leaving a long empty silence in the hall. It was several minutes before Bryony could speak, then she turned a dazed face towards Etta. 'Why did you do it?'

'I didn't do anything,' Etta wailed indignantly. 'Jeff really did phone, and he sent all those flowers. There was a card with them. Didn't you read it?'

'No. I — I thought they were all from Rafe.'

Her legs suddenly feeling weak, Bryony sat down on the stairs. Etta tottered over and joined her. They looked at each other dismally, then Bryony said tightly, 'Did you really lie about that letter from your old boyfriend?'

'No, of course I didn't,' Etta said crossly. 'I turned him down, so he must have decided to try to make a go of it with his wife. But he wasn't likely to tell Rafe that, now, was he? Especially if there was a possibility his wife might find out.'

'I'm glad to hear that.' They looked up as John Cornell came into the hall from where he'd been standing at the drawing-room door, out of their line of sight. Etta gave a small, dispirited sigh. 'I'm afraid we've heard most of what's been going on here. You weren't exactly keeping your voices down,' he said mildly. 'I guess I'll have to —'

The phone rang on the hall table. 'If that's that man Jeff again I'll give him a piece of my mind,' Etta said vehemently, getting to her feet.

'Tell him not to come here. Tell him I don't want to see him,' Bryony said quickly.

'No, no. You're not thinking straight.' John Cornell put out a hand to stop Etta as she reached for the receiver. 'Here, let me take the call.'

They were too bemused to protest, and listened dumbly as he answered. 'Jeff. Yes, I know who you are. No, she isn't back yet. Look, son, take my advice; get on a plane and come on over.'

He frowned and waved Bryony off as she gasped, 'No,' and came over as if to take the phone from him. Ignoring her, he went on,

'You're not going to get anywhere in a thing like this just sending messages, you know.' He listened. 'You'll take the first plane? Good for you, son. Just take a cab from the airport. See you tomorrow.'

As he put the phone down both women rushed forward.

'Why did you do that? You know I don't want to see him,' Bryony wailed in dismay.

'What have you got in mind?' Etta said more practically.

'The Count doesn't believe this guy Jeff wants to marry you,' John said. 'So let him come here and show everyone that he does.'

'And just how is Rafe supposed to find that out when he's sworn never to come near me again?' Bryony demanded indignantly. 'All you've done is to mess up my life even more.'

'I'm sure that we'll be able to think up a way,' Etta soothed.

'Perhaps we can help.' The three other ladies came out into the hall, their faces agog with interest and excitement.

Bryony took one look, groaned, and ran upstairs to her room. There she picked up the flower arrangements and started throwing them through the open window, then hurled the cut flowers after them until all the vases were empty. Except for one flower. Picking up Rafe's single, perfect rose, Bryony threw herself on the bed and wept.

It wasn't even eight in the morning before Jeff's taxi was tooting at the gates for Giovanni to come and open them. John Cornell met him while Etta came to wake Bryony.

'I don't want to see him,' she said stubbornly.

'Bryony, if you want to get Rafe back then you have to.'

'It's a ridiculous idea; if Rafe finds out he's going to hate me even more.'

'Can you think of a better one?' Etta demanded. 'Now get dressed. Here, put this on; it will show off your tan.' And she handed Bryony a pretty sundress.

Jeff was waiting for her outside on the terrace and got quickly to his feet when she appeared. 'Bryony.' He stepped forward and kissed her possessively. 'You look great.'

'Thank you. This is—quite a surprise.' She sat down at the table, not wanting him to touch her again.

'I've been trying to find you for weeks,' he told her, sitting down opposite. 'I finally found out where you were from your cousin and I came out here as soon as I could get away. I thought it best to come myself and not just write. I asked your parents where you were first, of course, but they wouldn't tell me. Probably

thought I didn't deserve a second chance. And they
were right, too. But the more I was away from you, the
more I missed you and wanted you, darling,' Jeff said
ardently, reaching out to take her hand.

'Don't call me that.' She took her hand away. 'Do
we have to discuss this now? I need a coffee,' she said
irritably, pouring one out.

'I thought you'd be pleased to see me.'

Her eyebrow rose cynically. 'Why?'

He looked at her and then nodded to himself. 'You're
still angry at me for leaving. But I needed some space,
Bryony; I told you that. I needed to be alone for a
while to make up my mind.'

'About what?'

'Whether I was ready for marriage,' he said on a
triumphant note, expecting her to be overwhelmed.

'And you decided that you were,' she guessed flatly.

'Yes.' Leaning forward, he gave her one of his most
charming smiles. Looking at him, Bryony wondered
detachedly what she had ever seen in him. He was so
transparent. Compared to Rafe he was just a piece of
quickly moulded plastic, whereas Rafe was the finest
cut crystal, his every facet shining and revealing hidden
depths. 'I want to marry you, Bryony. Did she tell you
that? The woman who took my message. I wanted you
to know why I was coming, that I'd made up my mind.'

'Really?' Bryony glanced out to sea and grew still. A
motorboat she recognised was coming into the bay.
Rafe come to collect the yacht. It had served him ill,
turning the tables on him so that he fell in love with
her. She wasn't surprised that he was taking it away so
quickly — she wouldn't be surprised if he didn't take it
out to sea and scuttle it, to drown the memories it
would always evoke.

She stood up, her body stiff with tension, but John

Cornell came out on to the terrace and touched her arm. 'I think you're wanted in the kitchen, Bryony.'

'What? Oh, yes. Excuse me.'

She ran gratefully inside, leaving Jeff and the American together, but instead of going to the kitchen ran upstairs to the landing window where she had a good view of the beach. The motorboat came in quickly and Rafe tied up at the jetty. Then, to her horror, Bryony saw John walk down to the beach — with Jeff at his side. All three men met up at the yacht and she saw Rafe's shoulders stiffen as John obviously introduced them. Then they all bent to have a look at the yacht's side where a hole showed just above the waterline. It looked as if the boat must have slipped one of its lines and beaten against a protruding timber on the jetty. Bryony stared, trying not to think the thoughts that were coming into her head, not to realise it was too much of a coincidence that Rafe should arrive to look at the damage on his boat just when Jeff was here.

John Cornell left the others and walked unhurriedly back to the house, going round the side towards the garage. Now that the two men were left alone together, it was obvious that Rafe was sizing Jeff up. The two began talking, although it looked as if Jeff was doing most of it. This isn't going to work. I just know this isn't going to work, Bryony kept thinking, her heart palpitating. But Rafe had no reason to suspect John Cornell, and Jeff, of course, was completely genuine. So he might, he just might be convinced of the truth.

John returned to the boat with Giovanni, both of them loaded up with tools and some pieces of wood that they started to hammer over the hole. Jeff looked on for a few minutes, but he kept glancing back towards the house, then impatiently left the others and walked up through the garden, into the house and to the hall.

'What was the matter with the boat?' Bryony asked, coming down the stairs to meet him.

'A hole in the planking.' Jeff caught her arm, saying eagerly, 'There's so much I want to say to you, so many plans to make.'

But Bryony said, 'What did you talk to Rafe about?'

Jeff frowned. 'The American?'

'No, the man with the boat.'

'Oh, the Italian. He was quite interested in us, as a matter of fact. It seems you mentioned me to him a few times,' he added smugly.

'Did you tell him why you were here?'

'He asked me straight out. I suppose, being related to the owner, he was afraid you would be leaving.' Jeff smiled. 'How soon can we get away from here, darling?'

She blinked at his cool assumption that he had only to offer marriage to make her give up everything and fall at his feet. 'You can leave as soon as you like. I won't be going with you.'

'You mean you can't get away? You're under contract for the summer or something?'

'I mean I don't want to marry you, Jeff. Thank you for the offer, but I have other plans.'

He gave her an uneasy look. 'You've hardly had time to think it over.'

'On the contrary, I had plenty of time to think after we split up, and I decided a long time ago that my future doesn't include you.'

His favourite 'little boy hurt' look that she had actually once been mad enough to give into came into his face. 'Are you sure — or is this just a way of getting back at me?'

Angry now, she said, 'Do I have to spell it out to you? I don't love you and I don't want to marry you. Just go home, Jeff, and forget all about me.'

His face hardened. 'You're making a big mistake in

acting like this, Bryony. I've said I'm sorry that we broke up. I'm not going to beg and plead, you know. And I haven't got time to hang around here while you extract your pound of flesh.'

'Then leave,' she said shortly.

'Yes, why don't you?' Rafe came through from the terrace and put a familiar hand on Bryony's shoulder. 'You're the past as far as Bryony is concerned.'

Jeff's head came up in surprise, to change to one of chagrin as he said, 'Oh, I see. So that's the way the wind blows. Well, you certainly didn't waste any time.' He looked round for his case, which was still on the floor where he'd left it. 'Where can I get a taxi?'

'Giovanni will drive you,' Bryony offered.

'I'll find him.' Rafe looked at her. 'You'll be OK?' he asked in Italian.

She nodded, not looking at him directly. When he'd gone she said with difficulty, 'I'll always remember our time together.'

'You loved me then.'

'Yes. I thought I did.'

'But now you know different?' She nodded and Jeff shrugged. 'Oh, well, you can't win 'em all, I suppose. It's my own fault; I should have snapped you up when I had the chance.' Leaning forward, he kissed her on the cheek as Rafe came back with Giovanni. 'Good luck, Bryony. I mean it.'

'Yes, I know you do. Thanks.'

She stood silhouetted in the doorway to watch them as they drove away, then stepped back into the hall to where Rafe waited for her.

'It seems I jumped to the wrong conclusions,' he said, his eyes warm. Holding out his hand to her, he said, 'Forgive me, *cara*?'

Becoming aware of movement, Bryony glanced round and saw that John and Etta were standing in the doorway to the terrace, that the three ladies were on the landing listening avidly and openly, and Maria was peeping round the kitchen door, all grinning at the success of their plot. Turning back to Rafe, she felt her heart swell with love, her body ache with it, but her voice was very calm as she said, 'Rafe, will you do something for me?'

'Of course. Anything,' he replied instantly.

'Then just go to hell!' And she ran past him and up to her room before all their mouths had stopped falling open in astonishment.

Rafe banged on her locked door, threatening to break it down, Etta tried pleading with her, and John Cornell persuading, but Bryony refused to come out until she was sure that Rafe had left.

'I thought the whole idea was to get him back,' Etta said in exasperation when she finally emerged.

'Men! They're all the same,' Bryony declared angrily. 'They think they can just crook their finger and you'll come running. Well, he can think again. Let Rafe find out what it's like to feel rejected.'

He rang her a dozen times a day, came round every evening, but she refused point-blank to see him or talk to him. And, fearing that he would sneak in at night again, Bryony went round the house until she found his way in — up a strong creeper on the side of the tower and across the roof to a skylight over the store-room. She had Giovanni cut down the creeper and put a bolt on the fanlight, but locked her door every night for good measure.

She didn't even leave the house for over two weeks, but then relented when she received an invitation to the Red Cross ball along with Etta and John Cornell. The latter was their only guest now, and was truly a guest, Etta having cancelled the rest of their bookings and closed the hotel. 'It wasn't because of Rafe,' Etta

assured her. 'I might as well tell you; I'm going to
marry John and go to America with him.'

'You'll lose the villa if you do,' Bryony pointed out.

'Yes, but John has promised to buy me another
house here, so that I can come back as often as I like.
And besides,' she added with a twinkle, 'I'll be able to
come and visit you and Rafe here at the villa, won't I?'

'I don't even want to speak to that arrogant swine
again, let alone marry him,' Bryony answered shortly.

But she bought the most beautiful dress to wear to
the ball. A dream of a dress in cream silk that was
simple yet sophisticated, and that showed off her figure
but was feminine, too. She put up her hair and added
flowers from the garden, looked in the mirror and knew
that she had never looked better.

They arrived at the old *palazzo* in Catania where the
ball was to be held, the home of the Princess they'd
met at the charity lunch. The car pulled into the
courtyard, taking its place behind others as the cream
of Sicilian society, the beautifully dressed women and
their escorts, alighted and stood in chattering groups
before going in to be presented. Their turn came and
they went up the wide steps into the arched stone
entrance hall. Rafe was waiting for her as she knew he
would be, overpoweringly handsome in his evening
suit, his eyes holding hers, sending her messages,
pleading, loving, laughing when she couldn't resist
smiling at him.

'Am I punished enough?' he demanded.

'I think so,' she agreed huskily.

'So may I?'

She nodded, suddenly shy, and put her hand in his.
'Yes, you may.'

His face lit, and he gave her a look of such love that
she would remember it all her life. He kissed her hand,
holding it tightly, the kiss a pledge, then straightened

up. 'Come then.' He led her into the ballroom where the Princess and her aristocratic helpers were waiting to receive the guests. Speaking very clearly, Rafe said, 'May I present Signorina Ferrers — my future wife?'

Welcome to Europe

SICILY — 'the Garden of Persephone'

The biggest island in the Mediterranean, Sicily has something for everyone. The cities and resorts have all the style and sophistication you'd expect in modern Italy, but you can also discover some of the most stunning and unspoilt scenery anywhere in Europe. Add that to thousands of years of turbulent history, and a people renowned for their friendliness, and you have a winning combination!

THE ROMANTIC PAST

The Saracens who conquered Sicily in the ninth century AD saw it as paradise — so it's not surprising that the island has been fought over for thousands of years. Greeks, Romans, Byzantines, Arabs, Normans, Spaniards and Austrians have all come and gone, and left their mark in cities, theatres, temples, cathedrals and castles — and in the many romantic legends which cling to this enchanted place. . .

In ancient times Sicily was known as the **Garden of Persephone** — it was from here that the beautiful young goddess of nature was abducted by **Hades**, the terrifying god of the underworld. Each year she was forced to spend six months in Hell with him, causing our winter, but she was allowed to return to the earth for the rest of the year. When she was released, in spring, the wild flowers for which the island is still famous began to bloom!

Sicily was also the home of the handsome young shepherd **Acis**, who was loved by the sea nymph **Galatea**. Poor Acis was killed by the jealous monster **Polyphemus**, and Galatea threw herself back into the sea in despair. Let's hope your romantic adventures in Sicily have a happier ending!

Slightly more modern lovers associated with the island are Shakespeare's **Beatrice** and **Benedick** — *Much Ado About Nothing* is set here, in the city of Messina — and **Lord Nelson** and his **Lady Hamilton**. The naval hero was made **Duke of Bronte**, a small town on Mount Etna, and given a castle there in 1799.

THE ROMANTIC PRESENT — pastimes for lovers. . .

Wherever you go in Sicily, it's impossible to miss the looming presence of **Mount Etna** — at eleven thousand feet, the largest active volcano in Europe. And it's a *very* active volcano! There have been over a hundred and forty eruptions, from the first we know about, in 475 BC, to the latest in 1992, in which the village of **Zafferana** was almost buried by a huge river of lava — despite the efforts of the Italian airforce, who bombed the flow in an attempt to divert it! This gives an extra spark of excitement to a holiday on Etna. . .

In winter, you can **ski** on the volcano; in summer, you shouldn't miss a drive up from the lush, beautiful lower slopes to the eerie, moon-like landscape nearer the summit, where nothing but brightly coloured wild flowers grows on the black lava. The views are magnificent—you can see the whole of Sicily, the mainland coast, and, on a clear day, the island of Malta to the south.

Lower down the mountain, the slopes are clustered with charming, sleepy villages where people invite you into their homes to buy delicious local **wine** and **honey**.

A highlight of any visit must be the famous resort of **Taormina**. Perched on its seven-hundred-foot cliff, this must surely be one of the most romantic and sensuous places in the world, especially in the early spring, when the air is heavy with the scent of almond blossom. It's been a fashionable place for a holiday ever since Greek times, but it was 'discovered' by the European aristocracy early this century—famous visitors include **Oscar Wilde** and **DH Lawrence**.

The modern-day tourist can browse in the wonderfully tempting shops—open late—have a delicious meal in an elegant outdoor restaurant. . .or simply sit, sip an aperitif, and watch the stylish jet-set crowd pass by. . .

If you should tire of the beautiful people, there's always the passion and spectacle of **opera** and **drama**, performed in the superb **Greek theatre**, with the azure sea and Mount Etna as a matchless backdrop.

At the end of May, Taormina has a fascinating three-day festival featuring colourful traditional puppet shows — *Teatro dei Pupi* — which still act out centuries-old battles between crusader knights and Saracen warriors, and medieval stories of courtly love. There's also dancing and folk songs in traditional costumes, and a spectacular parade. . .it's a real taste of the old Sicily.

Wherever you find yourself on the island, you must sample the local cuisine, which is famous for its freshness — and its spiciness! **Seafood** is a speciality, especially *pesce spada*, or swordfish, which simply melts in the mouth, and **sardines**, which are often combined with pasta, raisins, capers and pine-nuts to produce the delicious *pasta con sarde*.

The fertile soil of Mount Etna grows fruit and vegetables that taste better than you could ever have imagined — you must try the local oranges (*arancia*) and succulent black **olives**.

Sicilians have a famously sweet tooth, so if you love ice-cream and sinful cream cakes you've come to the right place! There's an enormous range of mouthwatering *gelati* made with fresh fruit, and the special fruit and sponge cake *cassata alla Siciliana* is not to be missed. *Mangia bene*!

Of course there's always **wine** to go with your meal, often made on the slopes of Etna, and with a unique taste from the volcanic soil — watch out for **Etna bianco** (white), **rosato** (rosé) and the fiery **rosso** (red) which is often served chilled. And why not take home some of the famous dessert wines, **Marsala** or **Malvasia**?

A trip to Sicily is a perfect opportunity for shopping. In the hill town of **Caltagirone** you'll find beautiful **pottery** — often in blue and yellow, it seems to echo the colours of the sky, sea and bright Mediterranean sun, so what better souvenir to remind you of your holiday? There's also delicate **embroidery** and, if you're lucky, Arab-style woven **rugs** — a legacy of the long-ago rulers of the island. For a gift that everyone can afford, and children will love, you'll find *fruta alla Martorana*: marzipan cleverly shaped to imitate fruit. . .and even plates of spaghetti!

DID YOU KNOW THAT. . .?

* Sicily is almost a **thousand square miles** in size.

* there are over a dozen small islands around the coast, including **Stromboli**, which you can climb at night to watch the volcano erupting — from above!

* although most Sicilians speak Italian as well, the **Sicilian dialect** is still widely spoken, and is almost a language in its own right.

* Sicily has been an **autonomous region** of Italy with its own parliament since the 1940s.

* The Italian currency is the **lira**.

* To say 'I love you' in Italian you whisper '*Ti amo*'.

Harlequin invites you to the most
romantic wedding of the season.

Rope the cowboy of your dreams in
Marry Me, Cowboy!

A collection of 4 brand-new stories,
celebrating weddings, written by:

New York Times bestselling author

JANET DAILEY

and favorite authors

Margaret Way
Anne McAllister
Susan Fox

Be sure not to miss Marry Me, Cowboy!
coming this April

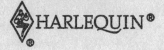 HARLEQUIN ®

MMC

HARLEQUIN®

Deceit, betrayal, murder

Join Harlequin's intrepid heroines, India Leigh
and Mary Hadfield, as they ferret out the truth
behind the mysterious goings-on in their
neighborhood. These two women are no milk-
and-water misses. In fact, they thrive on

MISCHIEF & MAYHEM

Watch for their incredible adventures in this
special two-book collection. Available in March,
wherever Harlequin books are sold.

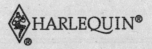

Where do you find hot Texas nights, smooth Texas charm and dangerously sexy cowboys?

Crystal Creek reverberates with the exciting rhythm of Texas. Each story features the rugged individuals who live and love in the Lone Star state.

"...Crystal Creek wonderfully evokes the hot days and steamy nights of a small Texas community...impossible to put down until the last page is turned." —*Romantic Times*

Praise for Bethany Campbell's *Rhinestone Cowboy*

"...this is a poignant, heart-warming story of love and redemption. One that Crystal Creek followers will wish to grab and hold on to." —*Affaire de Coeur*

"Bethany Campbell is surely one of the brightest stars of this series." —*Affaire de Coeur*

Don't miss the final book in this exciting series. Look for **LONESTAR STATE OF MIND** by BETHANY CAMPBELL

Available in February wherever Harlequin books are sold.